CALUM LOTT

First edition published in 2025 by Virtue Publishing

The moral right of the author has been asserted.

Word count: 42,961

Cover artist: John Devlin

Cover typography: Rachel St Clair (Claymore Covers)

ISBN: 978-1-7635181-4-8 (Ebook)

ISBN: 978-1-7635181-3-1 (Paperback)

ISBN: 978-1-7635181-5-5 (Hardcover)

To Hannah,
you make me a better man every day

CHAPTER ONE

Duel or Death

Nelsa steadied her trembling hands on the smooth grips of her pistolas. The bell tolled. She whipped out her guns, shot her opponent in the neck and chin, flicked the guns around her fingers a few times and slammed them down into the holsters. The body fell to the dungeon floor with a wet thump.

"And the winner is Nelsa Nolstar!"

The crowd erupted into a frenzy. Half the throng inside the packed room howled with laughing joy at their victorious champion. The others groaned and spat curses at the dead man wrongly wagered on. A few even started calling for violence.

Nelsa tightened her hands on the pistola grips to keep them from shaking, but that didn't stop the knot of dread she felt burning in her chest. The veroni withdrawals were in full swing. Her sloppy shots had missed their mark and not hit each of her opponent's eyes. One of these times her sloppiness would get her killed. Not tonight. Tonight she had won enough ismo to last her a few weeks. Veroni was a fairly cheap drink, after all.

She couldn't look away from the blood pooling around her dead opponent. A hateful scene replaced the duelling arena—a lifeless desert stained with the remnants of three lives. Each a different bloody size, though they all grieved her the same.

Nelsa shook herself free of the memory. She couldn't help that duelling was one of the only things she had a talent for—at least the easiest way of getting funds. But over the years she had become fine with killing in these duels for ismo. They attracted a certain sort.

Only now did the sting against her cheek register. Nelsa rubbed her fingers over where her opponent's blast had nicked her face and looked down at the blood on her hand. She let out a heavy exhale. It didn't matter that she didn't have her stala to protect her. She didn't care much about the prospect of dying in these duels. Death was no doubt what she deserved for getting them killed, but she could never give herself what she deserved.

A golden flicker snapped her mind back to the dull underground room. She blinked, but then caught the golden flicker again. A man stood dead calm amidst the raucous mob. A black hat covered his eyes. Pinned upon his chest was the golden crest of the Salazano Family—a planet with a blade piercing its surface. Something told her he wasn't there to wager on the duel.

Had she been found after all these years? She'd spliced herself to become an entirely different person. Whoever this enforcer of Salazano was, he was not here for her. It was nothing. It had to be. Regardless, she had to get out of there now.

The announcer glided over on his tall slender legs. "You never disappoint," he said, voice whispering like the rustle of a wind-blown forest. He placed his gleaming false hand upon her shoulder. "Are you sure there is nothing we can do to arrange a standing appointment?"

Nelsa craned her neck to look up at the tall illuavan and those large eyes that flared like swirling rainbow orbs of light. "Just send me the ismo," she muttered.

The illuavan flashed a row of narrow flat teeth, all gleaming an artificial gold. A deep pulsating growl warbled out the back of his throat and then his wide mouth closed. "Alright, alright," he said, scratching at the pale green skin on his cheek. "There you go. You just keep coming back whenever you need it. These scoundrels love your talents. Well, at least half of them do."

The ismo payment entered her thoughts like a river of lights passing through her skull. The corpus device embedded in her nape caught the signal and transferred the information to her brain. And there it was, like a replenished well of water, the funds to drown herself in numbness.

She brushed the announcer's shiny senyar hand off her shoulder and scurried past the flailing winners and losers towards the exit. Two humans guarded the steps with long blades pointed into the ground. She pulled the holster that contained the borrowed pistolas off her hips and handed them over. There wasn't any point in trying to keep them—they'd only had one shot each anyways. As she held them out, the solid weapons collapsed to a violet mist and drifted across to the swords, where they were reabsorbed.

The guards shuffled aside and Nelsa continued up the stairs. Her boots squelched on each slimy step and clung to her soles in gelatinous strands. She kept her hands in her pockets, fists clenched tight, away from the stained walls that reeked of a stagnant rot.

She stopped at the top of the stairs and looked about the room. Two more guards stood at the exit, quietly talking to themselves. A few other laughing patrons gathered on some half-decayed lounges, drinking, injecting, and inhaling a variety of substances in which she had no interest. Nelsa moved on.

"Well if it ain't our luck incarnate," one of the guards said. "What did I tell you, Ral? She's a true winner."

"You certainly know how to pick em, Taz." Ral shifted his blade to the side and stepped right up to her face. "Say, how come we only ever see you duel every other month? I miss those beautiful blue brown of yours."

"I don't miss yours," Nelsa said. "Let me through."

"C'mon," Ral said. "We'll be finished up here soon, then I can take you out for the night and treat you real nice."

"How about I take you out for a duel? I'd much prefer that. I can schedule you in for tomorrow. Unless you're ready now?"

Ral scoffed. "Your loss."

Nelsa brushed past him towards the security checkpoint, helped by a harsh nudge pushing her inside. Their laughter cut off as the door coalesced shut. She stood there in the small black room waiting. Her restless legs twitched every moment she wasn't given her stala and released. "What in the black void is takin so long?"

Several moments later, the plain black robes she and every patron were forced to wear down here collapsed to a dark mist and drifted away, reabsorbing into the walls. At the same time, a violet mist fell from the ceiling and swirled around her body until it solidified into her customised outfit. A black and green coat nearly touched the ground with black and white striped pants tucked into her tall boots. A dark corset wrapped above her waist and a white blouse covered her chest. A round hat hid most of her dark brown hair except for a few curly strands that framed her tanned narrow face.

Her anxiety lessened a notch now that she had her stala again—her ever present, malleable armour set. Even now it rapidly healed the bleeding scratch on her cheek. No stala could heal the wounds she gave her opponent.

Nelsa ran her mind through her stala, accounting for every single one of its cryluns, every minute organic machine. Whatever weapon her mind could conjure the cryluns would become. Such was this age of technology. And yet she was a woman of habit and always kept the same two pistolas hanging off each hip inside her coat.

The exit opened and she stormed out and up more steps bathed in darkness. The only light came from the blue glow of mad etchings scribbled all over the walls. She passed through another guarded door and finally reached the surface of Arkoma.

It was time to put her hard earned ismo to use. Time to drink some veroni and forget all about whoever she just killed and whoever that Salazano enforcer was. That was the only way she could endure living without her family. Numb.

CHAPTER TWO

Arkoma City

Arkoma City smacked Nelsa in the face with its claustrophobic liveliness and corrupted stench.

The bright lights. The cacophony of chatter, laughter, music and violence nauseated her. The worst offender was the reek of intoxicating serums that placated the vices of the city's inhabitants. The streets were packed with bodies flowing in either direction—a river she was loath to join.

Using the corpus linked to her brain, Nelsa connected to the city nexus and attempted to hail the grav-train. The option was unavailable due to engine repairs.

"For caosi's sake," she cursed. She knew Salazano just wanted to let everyone in the city—even the wealthy—know that he controlled them and could make their lives more difficult at any moment. Although perhaps he'd just allocated its use to some wealthy acquaintance to ride up to one of Arkoma's moons. Either way, taking away the only transport in the city meant that she had a long walk ahead of her.

Kayli always loved riding around in the grav-trains.

Whenever they lifted her up she would giggle with excitement. Nelsa had always admired her daughter's resilience when the Families shut them down for repairs or personal use. Even at eight years of age, Kayli never complained. Her gentle voice still echoed in Nelsa's mind today.

"'It's okay, mama,'" she would say, looking up at her with those big blue eyes. "'I still get to spend time with you.'"

Few precious memories lingered, but they only seemed to hurt more as the years went by. Despite that, she never erased them. That would have been worse than watching Kayli die all over again.

Nelsa could have used her stala to glide above the street and quickly get to her destination, but two lawkeeps passing by dissuaded her. Doing so was illegal in Arkoma and dealing with the lawkeeps was always a nuisance. Beyond that, her stala was too diminished. It did not have the strength left for flight, at least not far.

Nelsa looked past the lawkeeps and froze. A familiar figure stood inconspicuously across the street. His wide, tilted down hat made it so that she could only make out that thick moustache, but she knew who it was. Marston always seemed to be watching over her, especially of late. Growing more irritated by the second, she turned away and started walking down the busy artery of Arkoma City.

She kept her head low amongst the rushing crowd, one swift foot after the other. She occasionally looked back to see if the Salazano enforcer was following her, but she never saw any sign. Since the veroni had worn off right before the duel, her whole body pulsed with nerves, as though a serum of pure anxiety coursed through her veins. The mass of shifting bodies all around felt like a tempest of black guilt trying to trap her in her own frightened mind.

Her corpus connected to the city map and guided her to the closest saloon. She wouldn't be able to make the long walk to her favourite spot on the outskirts of the city, so settled for one nearby. Wealth slowly crept out from the lustrous inner sections in this strange middle ground of the city, whilst the rabble crept in from the slums.

Nelsa turned the next corner and winced from a mass of blinding fluorescent lights. Densely packed towers loomed on either side of the street. The lower halves were covered in bright signs, some of which were static, but most were moving and shaped into giant humans, illuavans and other beings all vying for attention. A scattered few reflective towers gleamed of the robust senyar material. The rest were grey bleak coffins that rose fifty levels into the night.

The Four Families left the Velutra centuries ago with all their senyar and their infinite nomismo and came to Arkoma. United, they quickly took control of the small established population and fashioned it to their desires. The Families only shared their senyar with those they deemed worthy, so they too could build equally graceful and sturdy structures.

The sight of two glowing red warlifs howling at one

another over a dark entry stopped her in her tracks. She'd walked by here with her son Colquin when he was just four years old. He pointed at the warlifs and asked what they were with bubbling curiosity. She'd lifted him into her arms and told him the truth: that they were fearsome beings with minds like humans, quick to anger, but capable of great loyalty and love. His light blue eyes had widened with innocent awe, then he sleepily nuzzled into her neck. She could feel the warmth there even now.

Only a week later she watched those curious eyes ruined by fear.

Nelsa swallowed the memory as best she could and continued walking with her head held high. Eventually she approached the saloon, but as she did so several warped screeches rang out across the street, followed by screaming and more blasts. The crowd broke out into a panic and everyone nearby scattered. Those who remained made a clear path in front of the disturbed tower's entry. Nelsa pushed her way through the crowd and stood on the edge, hoping the brawl in the saloon would be sorted out quickly so she could get inside and drink. Every time more screaming fire echoed out the horrified witnesses gasped.

Nelsa remained silent. And thirsty.

CHAPTER THREE

Law & Order

From above, three lawkeeps came down in grav-sheaths and landed safely in the clearing, each armed with heavy rifles. They were adorned in the black and gold outfit customary to the law and order Salazano employed. Long dark jackets covered their gold patterned vest, beneath which they wore dark pants and tall boots with gold chains wrapped around each ankle. Atop their heads sat circular dark hats with the golden Salazano pin.

"You come on out now with your stala relinquished, boy," one of the lawkeeps shouted, his voice projected by his stala.

"We know who you is, little Carlo," another lawkeep yelled. "Don't be makin this more difficult than it's already needin to be. We're gonna take you to your father, how's that sound? We ain't gonna hurt you."

"Filthy liars!" A whimpering voice cried out from inside the tower. "If any law takes a step in here I'll blow the life outta all these cowerin folk. Stay back!"

A wave of blasts fired out of the saloon but the

lawkeep summoned a translucent violet shield from the device on his wrist. They collided in high pitched grinding screams. There was no need to waste a perfectly strong stala.

Above the mayhem all Nelsa heard was the man's desperate voice ringing in her head, except now it was the father of her children as he fought off Salazano's assassins. The hopelessness triggered her memory of the bloody sands. The sorrow ensnared her for a moment and her twitching, restless body froze in remembered shock, but her ears kept listening to the altercation.

"You ain't gonna hurt anyone else," the lawkeep said. "Best use those wits of yours and think about this properly now."

A vessel slammed to a silent halt right above the clearing. It remained suspended there like a metal winged creature, hastily put together by a disfigured machine god. Three more lawkeeps fell to the ground and then issued orders for the gathered crowd to disperse as they established a larger perimeter. Nelsa remained in a daze of grief.

One lawkeep came right up to her and pointed the end of his golden barrel in her face. "Best you move along, friend. Lest you want what's comin to that fool in there."

Nelsa blinked and scowled at the lawkeep.

He laughed nervously. "You slow or somethin?" Then he gave her a quick look up and down and his jittery demeanour settled. "Nice stala you got there," he mocked. "It's so thin I'm surprised you can even put this pretty outfit together."

Nelsa's stala allowed her to perceive the thick transparent violet mist clinging to the lawkeep's body. Then she glanced down at her arms and legs. Her coloured field was noticeably thinner, even completely gone in several patches. She changed the filter so the stala became wholly invisible again.

The lawkeep tensely nudged the long barrel of his rifle closer to her face. "You really wanna be movin on."

She produced a smirking leer and took a slow step back. Then she spat at his feet and turned and walked away through the scampering crowd. Nelsa's corpus rerouted her to the next closest saloon, but when she came to the intersection, and looked left, the tower caught her attention like always.

Cutting through the bright gloom of Arkoma City stood Salazano's pride. Unhindered by other towers, this street stretched beyond what her eyes could see. All the way at the end rose a great black and golden pillar as though two coiled serpents were in battle to devour the sky itself. Every year the twisting serpents grew.

She turned away, but painted there on the closest building was a massive portrait of Malvatore Salazano himself. Depicted in an exorbitant chamber of polished black stone and gold jewels and servants, Salazano sat on his throne grinning over his dominion. He was the Padrino—the Lord of the Four Families in this region of the Frontier.

Nelsa thought back to her youth when the tower was jointly held by each leader of the Four Families and used as a place to convene and discuss matters pertaining to their sovereignty. But in his greed and strength, and the weakness of the others, Salazano took this tower as his own and made it far grander.

The reminders of Salazano filled her with that bottomless, uncouth rage like always. So many failed plans and cruel years spent trying to get her revenge just to end up where she started. Yet like always she didn't have the courage or strength left to fight.

Nelsa bowed her head and kept her eyes down on the filthy ground as she continued on. Numbing herself from all this suffering was the only thing she was good at anymore.

She hadn't got far when someone spoke. As if ten different humans were speaking at once, the deep layered voice caught her off guard. "You're making quite the name for yourself, Nelsa Nolstar."

CHAPTER FOUR

Propositions

Sitting unbothered amidst the busy street was a grey warlif. The creature rested on his two rear hinds, three tails spread out behind. The front two legs rose like pillars of midnight and supported a large furry head whose keen eyes burned emerald.

The warlif's snout shifted as his distorted voice rolled around like a violent dust storm before settling into a low rumbling growl of many pitches. "Having a notorious name is a dangerous thing in a city like Arkoma. Yet it can become a strength if you associate yourself with the right…friends."

"Who are you?" Nelsa demanded. "What do you want?"

A hail came to her mind and after a brief hesitation she curiously accepted. Her mind absorbed his words in an instant, thanks to her corpus.

"I come with a proposition you shall not find easy to refuse," the warlif said.

Nelsa clenched her teeth. *"I ain't wantin no part o' whatever this is,"* she replied.

The warlif bellowed a laugh. *"Do you enjoy those little duels? The scraps they feed you? The magnificence of your other talents can reward you far more. Or is it for the reckless risk of your life that you participate in them?"* The warlif's long snout gave a deep sniff. *"I can smell the despair leaking through your stala."*

Nelsa took a single step to the side and forward to move past the warlif.

"It's Salazano you hate, is it not?"

The warlif's words stopped her legs dead as though a grav-sheath had ensnared her. She could still feel the weight of the Salazano Tower gleaming golden above the warlif in the distance. In the depths of her vital, her being, her children and her love cried out for vengeance. Nelsa refocused on the warlif and his ears pointed up on alert.

She commanded her cloak aside to reveal her hands on her pistolas. Her thumbs rubbed over the smooth black handles with finely carved patterns. Between the long green barrel and handle gleamed a radiant orb which served as the pistola chamber, and stored the source that powered her stala. The chambers were currently small and faint as she had spent the last of her ismo on veroni instead of replenishing her diminished armour. Nonetheless, it still had a bit of strength left.

"You ever fought a warlif, lass? Those little things won't even tickle my senyar bones." The warlif let out a snarl, enticing her to give into the lust of battle. *"We could use that grand resentment of yours. You can stop these pathetic duels and have all the nomismo you'll ever need. You can get*

your revenge on Salazano. Then you can live in the numbness of the grief he has caused you, if you so choose it. What do you say?"

Nelsa glowered at the sound of the warlif's refined Velutran. She always found the language to be riddled with arrogance. Unbearable compared to the free-flowing way of talking that was most common throughout the Frontier.

"You ain't even here," she said. *"You're just projectin yourself through some poor fool in there."*

Nelsa flicked on her stala filter and the warlif's form became violet and misty, indicating that it was a projected form and not truly a warlif. She couldn't see through the disguise to the host. Her stala could create similar projections at full strength, but anyone with similar tech could see it was just a veil. To properly become someone or something else, one would need a chameleon.

"The human mind," the warlif laughed, *"so often trying to deny its true nature. If he had enough nomismo and the means, this poor fool would transfer his vital into a warlif body without hesitation. Why is your kind always fleeing from themselves?"*

"You forget you're born of our minds, cosless creature."

The warlif flashed his white daggered teeth, each as large as Nelsa's hands. *"Born yes, but also perfected."*

Nelsa's stala suddenly marked the same man with the golden pin who had been present at the duel. He lit a cig and put his back to her, but Nelsa knew he was watching. Fortunately, he couldn't hear the conversation between their minds. She wondered for a moment if Marston was still following her, but she couldn't see any sign. Besides, some part of her knew he had only been there to see if she'd made it out of the duel alive.

"*A lawkeep of Salazanos,*" the warlif said. "*He's been following you since your duel.*"

"*Why?*"

"*I told you before: having a notorious name is a dangerous thing in this city. Salazano will either want you for his own or put you down forever. I don't think you care for those two options, do you? But that is something I can certainly assist with.*"

"*And you ain't worried to be seen talkin to me like this?*"

"*Right now you're just talking to a nobody who thinks he's a warlif. The lawkeep is of little concern, but will be dealt with.*"

"*Just how long have you been watchin me?*"

"*Long enough.*"

"*What Family do you belong to? Your grudge against Salazano is clear enough. Your aura stinks of Ganava—or wait, no. You're from old Loyal Lecara. Yea, I can tell. You're his pet warlif, aren't you? That's why you took this form.*"

The warlif's tails twitched.

"*Little warlif pride couldn't help itself. Bad blood between the Families lately, ain't there? Salazano's tightenin his hold on y'alls throats. You have my deepest sympathies, best o' luck with it.*"

"*You need not worry about who I am or what Family I belong to,*" the warlif said with a mischievous rasp to his multi-layered voice. "*I'm just a messenger. You won't see me again after this. What you need to concern yourself with is my employer's offer."*

"Which is what exactly?"

"To put your talents to good use."

"I got no idea what you're talkin about," Nelsa answered firmly. *"The only thing I'm good at is killin fools in duels."*

"Duelling is a pointless skill in this age. Well, the killing aspect may prove useful. I was referring to the skills of you and your friends. Quite the elusive crew of thieves."

Nelsa felt a familiar sinking in her stomach. She tried her best not to show it on her face, but when the warlif's cold eyes narrowed, she knew that she had failed.

"You got the wrong person, friend."

"Nelsa Nolstar," the warlif continued, *"are you certain that's your real name? I'm not so convinced. There are few capable of splicing out here in the Frontier. You used to have blue eyes, didn't you, Layli? So did both of your children, Colquin and Kayli. Before they were slaughtered by Salazano."*

That sinking feeling turned into twisting dread and regret, churning up her throat as though she was about to retch. She squeezed her pistolas so tight she could have crushed the cryluns that held them together. Violence wasn't the answer right now.

"It is a fair hatred to bear after all these years and so I've come to offer you a sliver of revenge, if you want to take it."

The warlif didn't care who she was before or who she was now. She could find little reason for this to be some trap of Salazano himself, or one of the other Families. Anyone calling for harm against the Padrino would know the deadly consequences and be driven to proceed regardless.

Her grip eased off her pistolas. *"How do I know this is real?"*

"Is the offer of going against Salazano not enough? He has lost himself to greed and the ruling of others. The balance of the Four Families needs to be restored. It will be restored. But I thought someone with a disposition towards Salazano such as yours may like to be involved. I can send the necessary information to ease any doubts you may have, but I first need your word that you accept the task."

Nelsa folded her arms in contemplation. The temptation to get revenge on Salazano sounded more than appealing. Her very essence suddenly craved it, perhaps even more than a drink. *"Just what is it you need done?"*

"A heist."

CHAPTER FIVE

A Drink

Nelsa walked in contemplation for some time. A tentative plan and the players she'd need began to take shape, but the withdrawals eventually became too much to bear. Fortunately, the grav-train returned to service and dropped her right at the front of her favourite saloon in the outskirts of the city.

Just like the daily falling of Arkoma's Star below the desolate sandy horizon, she visited this saloon every night without fail. The appealing orange glow that emanated from the saloon's frosted windows made it feel like she was returning home. Nelsa pushed through the double swinging doors of the establishment and into the debauchery.

Her corpus connected to the saloon's system and accepted the entry contract. The quantum fluctuations constantly emitting from the grav-shield device in her pistola chambers ceased. There was no physical sign that anything had changed, except perhaps for the uneasy feeling of leaving herself open to artificial gravity attacks.

Nelsa had been cast out of a few saloons before, but had yet to tarnish her reputation at this one. Most establishments couldn't afford a grav-sheath, especially not out here in the outskirts, but this saloon was highly profitable and needed the extra protection. If any rowdy customers behaved poorly then the owner had the right to cast them out. That way no patron could seek satisfaction against the saloon afterwards for damages to their body or pride.

Entering the saloon punched her in the face with its raucous singing and laughter, but it was a welcome assault. The wet, thick scent of concoctions clung to every patron. Two women stood in the corner singing and the sapphire orbs in their hands caroled with a choir of upbeat accordion and piano melodies. The balcony upstairs swayed with a sea of dancing and drinking bodies and tightly packed tables filled the downstairs. Patrons gathered round each one, drinking and smoking and injecting and singing and gambling and laughing.

Passionate conversations prospered, some verging on violence. Well, violence currently erupted at one table, hushing the saloon, but the owner of the establishment quickly broke that up with the grav-sheath. It caught the offending parties in its transparent field and tossed them both past Nelsa out onto the street. Everyone laughed and promptly returned to their merriment, as did the music.

Nelsa's anxiety and obsessive thoughts already started slipping away. She was so close.

Unfazed by the disorder, Nelsa put one boot in front

of the other and moved deeper into the saloon. She eyed the long bar, crowded with swaying bodies being served by several barkeeps. Behind them stood a wall of colourful bottles containing a variety of vices. At the far left a single bottle gleamed amber. Void's Vapid Veroni. Her sin of choice. The perfect remedy to escape all her sorrow. That's where she headed.

She passed through the crowd of familiar faces. Most were human, a few coloured with the pale green of the illuavans, or the artificial glow of other projected beings.

Her eyes lingered upon a man sitting at the last row of tables. Marston "The Youngin" Devetta gave Nelsa a friendly tip of his curved hat. She glared in reply. Did he really think she wouldn't notice him following her, or did he just not care? But caring was the entire point. With his hand he brushed the thick hair over his smiling lip and returned to wagering on a game of faro. She had no care for. If she were going to try and win some ismo, she may as well gamble her life. It didn't matter if she lost that.

Marston called out to her as she passed, "Prosperous night, Nels?"

"You'd know, Mars," she mumbled, and didn't stop until she got to the bar.

Nelsa preferred to be alone in saloons and all the regulars there knew it, Marston included. That didn't stop him from watching her as she came in each night. There had been one evening a year ago when she allowed him to intrude and they got carried away.

In that brief moment of spontaneous company she'd felt the warmth and comfort of being back in the safety of Teec's arms, but Marston could never replace his loving embrace. She had assured him that it would never happen again. Despite this, they remained mostly cordial, as she occasionally counted on his ordnance expertise. Blowing things up wasn't her specialty when it came to thieving. Hers was planning and deception.

Nelsa found a vacant spot at the end of the bar. Her corpus connected to the establishment's network and formed a suspended seat as she plonked onto it with a weary exhale. Her hat misted into her high collar. She placed her elbows on the counter and brushed her hands through her dark brown hair.

One of the barkeeps stepped forward. "That time o' the night already is it?" he muttered through the pipe that hung from his mouth. He blew a trail of smoke that shot down to the bench top, swirled around for a few seconds, then dissipated, revealing a small glass gleaming with an amber liquid contents. "Why you're lookin especially thirsty this evenin. "

Thinking about the warm, acrid sensation of the veroni about to go down her throat kept her silent. She anxiously swallowed the saliva building in her mouth. Then her corpus sent the requested funds like a little river of light drifting away from her mind. She took the glass, threw it into her mouth, and slammed it back on the wooden bench. She tapped her fingers twice next to her empty glass.

The barkeep glowered then shook his hairless head.

A mist rose from behind the bench carrying an amber bottle. He grabbed it and poured the liquid. "Respect is a fadin thing these days, I tell you. Always a sorry, silent sight you are."

"Everyone's always got somethin to say," Nelsa muttered, taking the refilled glass in her hand and swirling it around. "No one can just keep their caosin thoughts to themselves."

"Not everyone only has bitter words to spew like you. Maybe I won't replenish my veroni wares next time. You're the only one who drinks this stuff anyways." The barkeep turned and left.

The numbing effects of the veroni began to kick in so she found it hard to care about whatever it was he said. She emptied the second glass. In truth, one was enough to last the entire night. The second was for good measure. Sometimes the veroni didn't numb those deep wounds that festered at the very centre of her vital.

The veroni hit her stomach with the heaviness of colliding planets. The blood pumping through her veins suddenly went cold. The dead feeling crept out from her stomach like a shadow of purgatory until all her limbs went so numb it felt as though…nothing.

She felt nothing.

Every night she would sit in the saloon numb and silent until starrise. Only when the veroni naturally wore off and she felt that slight tingle in her stomach would she stumble back to the filthy quarters she called home to force her mind into a dreamless sleep.

If only tonight hadn't been different.

CHAPTER SIX

Sippin on Misery

"Oi! You called me here!" a voice shouted. A distorted blend of the human and illuavan tongue splayed across several pitches. "Has that abused organic mind o' yours finally given in?"

Nelsa turned half-closed eyes to the glowing figure. Maasi floated like some bioluminescent jelly-type creature out of the depths of a deep and dark ocean. The coavlen had no eyes—zais entire form could perceive zais surroundings—but Nelsa always looked at Maasi's transparent domed head. Inside was a hidden cryluss core: the heart and artificial mind of a coavlen, made up of the same cryluss element that powered her stala. From this swaying head, many drooping tendrils glowed and flickered with different shades of blue, like half-frozen rivers in the sky.

Maasi sighed. "Are you gonna tell me what you hailed me here for or not?"

The coavlen might have been her only true friend left in the entire Frontier, except Marston. But that was different.

In a numb daze, she'd completely forgotten about hailing Maasi. Nelsa rummaged through her mind to find the information the warlif had given her about the heist and sent it to Maasi.

"This feels wrong," Maasi said, the words instantly arriving in Nelsa's mind. It was essential to not say specific things aloud. They never knew who was listening on Arkoma, especially in a crowded place like this. *"One o' those other Families is up to somethin. A long-lost heirloom that belongs to Salazano is comin all the way from the Velutra and someone wants us to steal it? What if it's some kinda new weapon or somethin?"* Maasi paused. *"You know what happened last time you stole from Salazano. Why would you want to do such a thing again?"*

"What does it matter?" Nelsa replied. When she thought of her family she felt nothing. *"You want the ismo, don't ya?"*

"How are we supposed to steal somethin if we don't know what it is? It could be anythin."

"It'll be the only thing on that coscraft of importance," Nelsa mumbled in thought.

"That's the thing innit?" Maasi said. *"Stealin somethin right in the presence of Salazano himself is a death warrant. He'll have every lawkeep flock to him. No, this feels like some kinda ploy by whatever Family is gonna pay us so they can mess with Salazano."*

"It don't matter to you nor the ismo that'll flow to ya. All we have to do is hand over the heirloom. Are you in or not?"

"Course I am, you human muck," Maasi said. *"Can't let you have all that sweet ismo. So, you put together a plan yet*

or just been sippin on veroni and misery?"

"Got an idea or two."

"Go on then."

Before she could cast her plan to Maasi through thought, her stala warned of a man rushing up behind her.

"You deceivin, thievin, no good sand-dwellin bottom-feeder!" he shouted, slurring every word. "I want a refund on that display you just put on. I challenge you and demand satisfaction!"

Maasi chuckled. "A new friend of yours?"

Nelsa drew a deep breath and the chair spun her around. She shifted her jaw and her half-closed, red-cracked eyes stared blankly at the short, gaunt-faced man. Her harsh countenance told him to move on lest he wanted a hole in his head, but the man took another step forward.

"You're in league with that illuavan announcer, ain't you?" He shot a finger forward. "Always makin a fool outta all us wagerin folk. You should be ashamed of yourself! I'll shame you aight. Outside. Right now."

Nelsa's eyes slowly scanned the wobbling man up and down. "You best walk away, friend, lest you want to keep havin regrets."

"I don't give a caosi, friend! You owe me what's been stolen!"

The patrons caught on now and the saloon fell quiet. Keeping her eyes on the man, Nelsa's stala scanned for any other threats. There were none. Marston still sat at his table, those stony eyes fixated on the man, as was the pistola he held in his hands. She realised it had been there since the man first approached. Marston was always good back-up.

"I ain't done no robbin," Nelsa said. "I won those duels fair, that's the truth. Best you go back to whatever hole you stumbled up from and keep on drinkin that bottle o' starshine, friend."

The barkeep stepped closer to the disturbance. "You both take this outta here now, lest I cast ye out mah self!"

The man stamped a wobbling foot on the ground. Turning to the rest of the saloon, he screamed, "I demand satisfaction! All ye bear wit—"

With his back turned to her, Nelsa sluggishly drew her pistola from the holster on her hip and fired two shots up into the man's neck. One blast broke through his weak robes—far weaker than even her barely intact stala. The second blast broke through his fragile flesh and gave him the satisfaction of death that he so desperately craved.

The blast obliterated the man's neck, sending his limp body and severed head flying across the saloon to land atop the nearest table where Marston sat. The head would have spoiled their beverages and game but the crylun cups and projection were accustomed to frequent disturbances and protected themselves. A light drizzle of blood fell in the path of the travelling head. The slightly aghast patrons of the saloon made no movement or sound. They knew what came next.

"Not in my saloon you don't!" the barkeep bellowed.

CHAPTER SEVEN

Plucking Stars

The cosmic power of a grav-sheath clenched Nelsa in its grip and tossed her out of the saloon. Her stala failed to properly protect her as she picked up cuts and bruises while rolling across the harsh orange dirt road. Not that she felt them. The veroni still had her in its grasp. The grav-sheath could have torn both her legs off and she would have felt nothing.

She lay in the middle of the dusty street looking up. There were no grand and elegant towers in the outskirts of Arkoma City, just cheap low-storied buildings like the saloon. From here she could see a faint field of stars shimmering through the hazy black sky. A pale red moon gleamed low on the horizon, but a blue illumination suddenly bathed her face with light.

"The drinkin is one thing," Maasi said, that contorted voice deep with disapproval. "But what are you doin killin nobodies like that for?"

"The Frontier is better off without him," Nelsa droned. "I seen that cretin shootin up a poor fella in cold blood just last week and he's always up in the saloons pesterin the women. He deserved it. Besides, he should have wagered on me."

"You're lucky the law doesn't come out this far for simple killin like this, least not urgently. And I ain't gonna argue with him bein sent to the black locker, but you ain't no lawkeep. I don't concur with you doin the killin. Does your vital no good. Yours already has enough to worry about."

"You don't know nothin, coavlen. You ain't bound to this real world like me."

Nelsa rolled her head to the side and saw the judgement in the eyes and laughter of a few people leaving the saloon. Fortunately, the veroni also kept away the shame of being thrown out of her favourite establishment.

"Flush yourself clean of the veroni," Maasi said. "You want to do this thing and not on your own? Then you best hurry it up. I ain't talkin to you anymore in this state. "

"What's it matter to you what state I'm in?"

"I'm tired of all your wallowin. I hear your words, but it's like you ain't even here. I can't keep watchin you hide and rot yourself, that's what's the matter. Now flush yourself clean with a serum, or I'll do it for you."

"It's like I hear your words," Nelsa said, "but I ain't gonna heed em. Besides, I ain't got no—" Before she could react, Maasi wrapped zais glowing tentacles around Nelsa's left forearm and shattered the weak stala there. The closest parts of Nelsa's clothing collapsed to a violet blur and rushed to defend her, but it was too slow. A sharp bite of pain pierced her arm. Maasi retracted the stala needle and released zais grip, drifting backwards.

The cold rush spread from her arm across her body and the heavy weight of existence hit her like a crashing meteor. She grunted and shot up to a sitting position. Her jittery limbs ached.

"Well," Maasi said, "since you still haven't learned to carry sobriety serums like I keep tellin you, I figured I best keep them stocked myself."

Nelsa glared up at the coavlen. "You've got some nerve," she panted.

"Tens of thousands of nerves, thank you very much. Or did you already forget that I'm a cosless coavlen?"

Nelsa scoffed then looked away, wincing. She lifted both her hands up and rubbed her palms against her face as though waking from a long slumber. The burning knot in her chest returned and the scene of her family's massacre flashed before her drowsy eyes. Instead of the usual dominating grief, anger stirred within. Salazano. This heist was the only way she could get her vengeance.

Nelsa rubbed her neck and looked around. The streets were quiet with only a few passersby who paid her little attention. Those who lived in the outskirts cared little about their appearances. Fashion was far less important and less refined compared to the Family loyalists who dwelt closer to the heart of Arkoma City in their fine suits. The men out here dressed in long dull pants and shirts, tall boots and wide-brimmed hats, while the women wore long flared dresses and lengthy curled hair.

Nelsa's left arm and shoulder were unclothed and unprotected by her stala now. She wasn't one to wear clothes underneath—most didn't. There wasn't really any point if you kept your stala replenished.

"We good?" Maasi asked, an air of mischief in zais voice.

Nelsa glowered up at the floating translucent jelly that was her friend. She knew she had a problem and Maasi was only trying to help, but she could never stay away from the veroni for long. Nelsa could not deny that it felt nice to have someone other than Marston looking out for her wellbeing. Even if it was just to earn zais share of the heist.

"Yea," she said. "We're good."

"Now then." The coavlen changed to speaking over their corpus link. *"Based on your plan, we're gonna need a Slippery Belle."*

"I thought you could be our very own."

"May as well just do everythin on my own then," Maasi said.

Nelsa got to her feet with a weary sigh. *"Alright, we need a Slippery Belle. Any thoughts who?"*

"Quake is our best option, but she's out Bazabarni way."

"We don't got the time for her to travel all that way here. This heist needs to happen within the week."

"Well, we don't talk to Runner, not since...you know. I'm afraid we ain't got no one else to be our Slippery Belle. Our circle is small these days, Nel, you know that. Talent in this city is limited. The only others that are somewhat in it are..."

"They ain't no Slippery Belle, that's for sure," Nelsa

answered. *"They'll take one step in there and light up the entire tower. And they just so happen to be a major drain on my vital."*

"StarFlower and MoonKidd are all we got," Maasi said. *"They're our friends, Nel. I reckon they can handle it."*

The rowdy duo always got it done, but half the time they didn't follow the plan and ended up putting everyone else in danger. This heist needed to be perfect. Nelsa wanted to keep searching for someone else, but the black and gold glimmer of the distant Salazano Tower stole her attention. It loomed over everything. But from way out here she could see that it indeed had an end. The rising coiling serpents did not go on forever. Nothing did. This might be her last opportunity to get back at Salazano, and she couldn't let it slip through her grasp. She owed it to herself and her family.

Clenching her fist, Nelsa felt some strength left. *"Aight, I know where we should be able to find em. They're always in the city. But you're gonna be responsible for keepin em in line this time."*

"I'll probably have a better chance of tryin to reach up and pluck one of those stars from the sky."

"Yea well, pluck a few. We're gonna need Costhrall on this one."

Nelsa looked past Maasi and saw Marston striding over. One hand fiddled with his hat, whilst the other rested behind his back. "Why is it that every time I see both of you together I get a sense that my ismo will soon be replenished?" He titled his hat back to show his thick moustache failing to hide his smile. "So, what's the job?"

CHAPTER EIGHT

The Hand of Chaos

"Well I've found em," Maasi said. *"Though I ain't so sure you want to know any more."*

In the morning starlight, Nelsa stared off to the other side of the eatery. Two parents were laughing at one of their children making silly faces, while the other two youths gulped down their meals.

She hardly touched her own food. Maasi had made her purchase it. She didn't really eat anymore—most of the time she relied on nutrient injections to keep her shell of a body operating. She only wished the meal came with a fresh glass of veroni. Maasi had also forced her to drink tea, and she couldn't admit to the coavlen that it was actually steadying the withdrawals as zai promised.

Nelsa roused out of her daze. *"Show me."* A small cloud of the coavlen's modified cryluns had found the location and quite cunningly, as Maasi was prone to be, slipped through their defences and took a peek. The image suddenly appeared in Nelsa's mind as clear as if she were there.

StarFlower and MoonKidd were held upside down

in the semi-transparent air of a grav-sheath. They had been stripped of their stalas. Their naked bodies were covered in bleeding wounds which slowly spilt out and hung around them like tunnelling worms of blood.

"I told ya, didn't I?" Nelsa growled in thought. *"A drain on my vital. What happened to em?"*

"They tried to steal a coscraft from an associate of Salazano's," Maasi said. *"The maniacs sent twelve law to the abyssal locker before they were caught. It seems they were gifted to Salazano's favourite servant."*

A figure stepped from the shadows. She recognised those dangling gold earrings of the Sal Family Crest. Vatore "Vital Scream" Belva, the Hand of Chaos. His pale face had cavernous dark holes where eyes should have been. Despite this he stalked around his trapped prey, his corpus directly guiding his mind rather than sight.

Nelsa's mind flashed to the deserts beyond Arkoma City. The assassin circled her family, pinned against the scalding sands. Their cries echoed throughout her vital like the toll of the sacred duelling bell. She shook the sounds and images away. She had enough anger to keep her going. She couldn't let herself sink back into the grief.

Her rage fixated on Belva. All Nelsa could think about was putting a nice big hole through his skull. Then she'd jam her fist in through the bloody cavity and swing his corpse in a message to Salazano. Belva was just a thrall, after all. A pathetic sort whose foul mind was enslaved to Malnetha, defiling the cosmos in any way possible.

Salazano was Malnetha itself to her.

"We have to get em outta there," Nelsa said. *"They won't have much longer left if we don't."*

She pushed herself up from her seat at the eatery and started marching down the street in the direction of one of Belva's many torture dungeons. Everyone in her circle knew about their existence. Void, everyone in the entire city probably knew; the fear was just another way Salazano kept his stranglehold. The public hangings also helped. If that kid she'd seen earlier shooting up the saloon wasn't killed in his arrest then he'd be strung up somewhere in the city.

"We can't just storm a Salazano hideout!" Maasi cried in thought. The floating coavlen swiftly caught up to Nelsa.

"I ain't gonna let Belva kill them! Now how many they got in there?"

There was a slight delay before Maasi answered. *"Five I can count, includin Belva, all with full stalas. That's not what even concerns me. It's the hundred they can hail to be there in a minute. We're thieves, Nel. We plan and then execute. We don't just go rushin in like Malnetha-raisin fools."*

"We're thieves," Nelsa repeated. *"We adapt through improvisation."*

"Even if we broke them out with our lives intact, StarFlower and MoonKidd are gonna have every lawkeep in the city lookin for em. They won't be able to move freely and neither will we!"

"*Sounds like they could be used for the perfect distraction if you ask me.*"

"*You would toss them out so easily into the void?*"

"*We'll get those new chameleons off Jasolle. They'd hide us just fine, I reckon.*"

"*And where in the blighted Malthezuul are you gonna get enough ismo to buy five chameleons?*"

"*Well I got a little from that duel, but Jasolle owes me a score or two.*"

"*A score or two don't seem equal to five chameleons. You're always relyin on his funds to bail you out. That ocean is gonna dry up one of these days and you're gonna die thirsty.*"

"*Yeah, well I've drank my fill, it don't matter how I die now.*"

Nelsa could feel the coavlen's condemnation leaking through their corpus connection.

A grav-train silently soared above them in a black flash, indetectable if it weren't for her stala's keen observational abilities. Ahead of them, descending just as swiftly as the train passed overhead, a human wreathed in a grav-sheath fell safely to the ground. The faint ovoid barrier vanished and they continued walking down the street.

"*We don't got no choice,*" Nelsa said. "*Belva likes to take his time when he's free to torture, but they are still gonna meet a cruel end. I can't let that happen, Maasi.*"

"*Ain't you just say how they're a drain on your vital?*"

"*They're still my friends.*"

"*They're mine too. I'm just tryin to avoid gettin us all killed.*"

"I got a plan. Well, the outline of one."

"Spill it," Maasi said.

Nelsa hailed Marston and added him to their connection.

"Did you find em?" he asked.

"Yea," Nelsa said. *"Belva's got em."*

"Oh cos, that ain't good. Well what are we goin to do?"

"We need your speciality of makin things go BOOM."

CHAPTER NINE

Breakout

Nelsa leant against the partition and gazed out the grav-train window at the rapidly moving city below. One minute they passed over dull, square towers, the next the hardly discernible poor buildings of the outskirts covered in the orange dust of the desert, then the gleaming senyar towers of the inner city, before the train circled back around and the view repeated.

Nelsa turned away from the stark reminder of this city's corruption and rubbed her eyes. She hadn't drunk any veroni since Maasi flushed her clean last night. Though the tea she'd drank at the eatery helped calm the shakes and anxiety, having a drink was all she could think about. It melted into every thought. Nelsa usually slept through the days. She would spend them curled up in a forced, dreamless sleep. But she had to focus on planning the heist, which first meant rescuing StarFlower and MoonKidd. She would get back to numbing herself soon enough. There was no denying that.

"*You got control o' this thing yet or what?*" Nelsa said.

"*Of course,*" Maasi answered. "*We're good to go on the*

train's next pass. One minute. Let's hope they don't figure it out until then. Jasolle's place is all nice and cosy waitin for you. Let's hope you can make it here in one piece."

"I told you he owed me a score or two and would help us."

"Yeah, and then he vanished for some 'meetin.' Gettin himself out of harm's way should the law catch us here, that's what that is."

"He's got to protect his interests," Nelsa said. *"We ain't the only ones he helps from time to time."*

"I know," Maasi said. *"Shame those chameleons weren't ready. At least he replenished your stala."* Nelsa glanced down at the translucent purple veil protecting her. No exposed patches anymore. Her thoughts drifted to Maasi, who coordinated their operation from the confines of Jasolle's safehouse in the outskirts. She was sure she left a vial of veroni or two the last time she was there. Maasi wouldn't be able to force a serum upon her now with a renewed stala.

Nelsa shook the thought away. She needed to focus. *"Marston, you good?"*

"Bombs are ready to give Belva a fright and the corpus drone is in place for you to scoop em up. Say, you think they'd rescue one of us if we were in the same situation?"

"They would if they needed us for somethin," Nelsa said.

"Ain't that the truth o' the world," Maasi said. *"A whole lotta back scratchin."*

"You don't have a back to scratch, Maasi."

"Why thank you for the reminder on the account o' my bein not naturally born in this cosmos."

"Why it's been mah pleasure," Nelsa said, allowing a

small smile to grace her hard face.

"Every lawkeep and bounty collector in the Frontier will be huntin your faces in a few short moments," Marston added.

"Better that than knowin I left StarFlower and MoonKidd to a torturous fate. Aight, focus up. Time to do this."

Through Maasi, Nelsa watched as the small mist of cryluns spying on their captive friends now moved to infiltrate the dungeon's defences. They chewed through the walls like tiny acidic mites dissolving stone until they reached the grav-sheath system. Then they seeped into the sphere of violet plasma containing the veiled heart of the gravity harnessing machines, unleashing their hostile programming. The machines emitted an increasingly loud whir before they went silent. The plasma sealing the reactor inside collapsed, rendering it dead. The grav-prison holding Starflower and MoonKidd vanished and they fell to the floor in a rain of their own stagnant blood.

"Marston, now!" Maasi cried.

"Time to send forth mah little pet," Marston answered.

In another corner of her mind, Nelsa watched a flying black serpent no bigger than herself dart over a short building. It opened its wide jaw and its fangs lunged down, biting into the centre of the flat roof. The wriggling body of the organic machine suddenly glowed a violent crimson. The head of the pulsating serpent collapsed in on itself and a blast chewed through the building, reducing everything in a well-defined circular pillar to mere particles. Marston had told Nelsa beforehand that there was a thirty-percent chance the blast would kill the prisoners, a risk she willingly took. A quick death like that would be a mercy compared to Belva.

Barely a second after the blast, a small drone flew over the opening and cast down two silver bands in grav-sheaths. They collided with the prisoners, wrapping around their necks. Marston remotely controlled the craft and then flew it away from the city and the lawkeeps that would shortly be in pursuit.

Another second later the flying train—controlled by Maasi—passed directly over the building's newly formed vertical entryway. The train connected to the external corpuses wrapped around their necks and spawned a grav-sheath around their prone bodies. Then they were lifted all the way back up through the sky to land right beside Nelsa in mere seconds.

"Thought y'all could use a helpin hand," Nelsa said, their minds now connected to the joint channel.

Starflower and MoonKidd stood in the grav-train, naked and covered in bleeding wounds. Fortunately Belva hadn't done much more to them in the last few hours. The pair's fright quickly turned into elated surprise.

"Nel!" Starflower cried. The massive human was defined by muscle and a thick hairless head covered in red runes. He rushed forward and squeezed her in a tight embrace.

"Take these stalas and cover yourself, would ye?" Nelsa shouted into their minds.

StarFlower took a step back and Nelsa pulled out two violet spheres that broke into a mist. One drifted over to cover him in plain black robes and seal his wounds.

Nelsa turned to MoonKidd. *"My my, it's only been a couple of months. Have you grown or is it just my eyes?"*

MoonKidd scowled back. *"I'll let that slide, seein as you just broke us out and all."* The salenai was less than half Nelsa's size, covered in more distinct muscles than StarFlower, except they appeared on the outside of her desert red skin. Her new stala covered her in similar dark robes and it reorganised her messy hair into two long braids on either side, one a ruby red, the other a void black.

"My bad," Nelsa said. *"I think it's just your new hair-style."*

MoonKidd didn't respond this time. Her mischievous eyes, the same colours as her hair, scanned the passengers in the semi-open carriage.

Nelsa looked about and saw the disdain in their curled mouths. Even she had seen stranger things when going around the city transport. Then the eyes of one passenger went wide and his head moved in panic from side to side. He'd realised that he was unable to cast himself down to the surface and was trapped in the moving grav-train.

From her stala, MoonKidd formed a handcannon thrice the size of her small red hands and pointed it at the closest two passengers. "Your ismo, give it up now!"

"Oi," Nelsa cried. "What the caosi are you doin?"

MoonKidd grinned. *"You've taken control of the train*

haven't you? These poor fools can't escape, so I'm gettin paid." Her rough voice raised into shouts. "All ye listen up! This is a robbery and you will oblige!"

Nelsa let out a scoff as the passengers started to scream and scramble down the carriage, except for a few frozen with fear.

"I break you out and the first thing you do is stick a gun in someone's face? I shoulda left you down there with Belva."

MoonKidd chuckled. *"No use dwellin on the past. We're here now and thrivin."* She stepped forward pointing the massive handcannon in the faces of the hostages and shouted: "I ain't gonna ask for your ismo again. Empty those minds now. C'mon, we don't got all day."

CHAPTER TEN

Spankin the Law

"Thanks for the rescue," Starflower said. *"But how you gonna get us outta here? You do have a plan, right?"*

"Gotta wait till we can cast out at the right spot," Nelsa hastily responded. She glanced out the window at the swiftly moving city below. *"Hopefully before Belva or the law retakes control of this thing."* Maasi's connection showed the four lawkeeps stationed aboard rushing towards their carriage.

Once MoonKidd collected her funds, the newly self-appointed robber pushed one of the hostages out into the main corridor and screamed, "You come any closer and I'll blow this upstandin citizen's head into oblivion!"

A wave of blasts barreled down the corridor, striking the hostage in three places. His weak citizen's stala blocked the first one, but the next two chewed through his flesh, one in his chest and the other in his thigh. He gave an immediate cry of pain, at which point MoonKidd pulled him back into their cabin.

"You forget who we're dealin with ya fool!" Nelsa

cried. *"Why are you always tryna get our own folk killed?"* She cast off a mist of her own stala to help seal the wounds of the bleeding passenger. He was already unconscious, but he would survive with her help.

"That's my bad," MoonKidd admitted. "The ol lust of breakin free got hold of me." She took a step closer to the unconscious man. "I apologise profusely, sir. Do you hear me? Do you accept or seek reparations?"

Nelsa shook her head in disbelief. *"Priorities! Would you mind keepin the approachin law busy without gettin folk shot? Can you at least do that?"*

"Aight, aight," MoonKidd said, backing away. "Quit your hollerin." She moved to the edge of the cabin and StarFlower followed. She looked up at the big man. "What ya thinkin? Time for an old lumenshield and switch?" Starflower smiled and nodded down at her.

MoonKidd summoned a lumenshield from the external device around her neck and the translucent violet sphere followed her as she leapt out into the hallway. With a handcannon in each hand, she pointed them in opposite directions and started blasting at the law from the protection of her shield. "Yeeehawww!" she shouted. "You take that spankin, law!"

Screeches banged against her shield in return. It would hold for a while before it shattered. From his own stala, StarFlower formed and tossed two cannons into the hallway whilst he stayed inside the cabin. The cannon's quad barrels whirred as they spewed forth crylun blasts.

In that moment Nelsa remembered the pair's usefulness.

"*Twenty seconds till the drop,*" Maasi said.

MoonKidd laughed in a frenzy. "They're comin up with blades!"

"They want to give us quick deaths," StarFlower grumbled.

Nelsa looked at the two huddled passengers in the cabin, but all she saw was the fear in their eyes. She'd seen that same fear in her family's eyes. She tried her best to give these passengers the comfort she couldn't give them. "You ain't gonna be harmed," she said. "*Maasi, cast them outta here!*"

A moment later a bubble of distorted space covered the two hostages and the unconscious one. Then the floor beneath them rippled and they vanished in a blur as they were safely cast down to the surface.

Nelsa's stala alerted her to the opposite end of the cabin. Several golden blades were cutting an entrance through the senyar walls. She whipped herself around and drew both pistolas from their holsters. Shaping them with her mind, a misty violet blade grew out along the barrel of each pistola, grips shifting into a straight hilt. If one got into any kind of fighting in the Frontier it was best to know how to wield a blade as well—that's where the real difference between life and death began.

The lawkeep finished carving his way in and the loose piece of wall suddenly launched forward at Nelsa. It crashed against her spawned lumenshield and fell to the floor with a heavy metallic thud. The lawkeep flung himself in next and brought dual golden blades down upon her shield, one strike after the other. Nelsa held both her pistola blades together. Pouring a solid amount of cryluss from the glowing orbs hanging off her hips, she fired a heavy blast that smote the attacker in the chest and sent him flying back into the opposite cabin.

Outside in the hallway, thunder rumbled throughout the train as MoonKidd's shield shattered. StarFlower spawned his while hers went on cooldown. The big man leapt from the cabin into the hallway, positioning his back against MoonKidd's with both of them under the shield's protection. He collapsed his two firing cannons into mist and formed them into a massive mace in his hands. When the next lawkeep attacked the edge of their shield, StarFlower turned and swung his spiked bludgeon. The law flew back down the corridor.

The salenai merged her two handcannons into a short-barreled shotgun and fired a heavy blast at the closest attacker. *"I ain't got much of this stala left to spank the law with,"* she said. *"How many seconds did you say again, Maasi?"*

"Ten!" the coavlen answered. *"Make sure you're all standin where I can cast ye down!"*

Outside, two coscrafts approached to intercept the grav-train. The quantum fluctuations of the train prevented the law from ripping Nelsa out with their artificial grav systems. They could have blown the grav-train out of the sky but Salazano only had four. Each was precious. Besides, plenty of civilians remained on board. Despite the law's carefree attitude towards civilian life, murdering an entire train of them was different than a hostage or two getting caught in the crossfire. The coscrafts opened fire on Nelsa's cabin, but Maasi had already powered up the train's lumenshield, absorbing the damage.

The lawkeep Nelsa had sent flying back quickly recovered. He tossed one of his blades straight at her shield and they screeched against each other for a drawn-out second before the blade collapsed. Nelsa fired blasts from her pistola blades. They blew chunks off his stala, made visible by violet ripples of mist and that sharp metallic sound. He tossed his other blade and her shield shattered with a crack of thunder. The lawkeep formed two more blades from his reserves and leapt forward. Nelsa rushed towards him.

Her crossed blades met one of his, screaming cryluns destroying one another. His other blade came in for a quick low thrust at her stomach. Unable to dodge, her stala took the blow, saving her from feeling any pain. But a few more hits like that and she'd be feeling the pain alright, if she could feel at all.

"*You ready or what, Maasi?*" Nelsa yelled, clenching her teeth against the heaviness of their clashing blades. It felt as though the weight of a star pushed against her.

"*Almost there!*"

"*Before they decide to just blast the entire train outta the sky would be nice!*"

"*Get ready for the drop! Three!*"

MoonKidd and StarFlower broke off and darted back into the cabin.

"*Two!*"

Nelsa summoned the remainder of her cryluss into her blades and that enhanced strength allowed her to push the lawkeep away.

"One!"

Nelsa felt that familiar sensation of the universe clenching her in its grasp and casting her down through the floor of the train towards the planet's surface.

The world rolled around in a blur.

The next moment everything darkened as she was released from the grav-sheath. Her boots sloshed in the filthy water of the sewers beneath Arkoma City. StarFlower and MoonKidd stood nearby.

"One of your finer rescues," MoonKidd said.

"We ain't out of it yet," Nelsa replied. A shaft of light beamed down through the wide hole in the tunnel Marston had previously created. In the surrounding darkness she marked several glowing red spheres attached to the walls. *"After me, and quick!"*

Her stala lifted her off the ground and she flew down the dark tunnel, the pair following her. They hadn't got far when Nelsa triggered the glowing spheres. They ejected a disrupting field to confuse any pursuers.

"You are one mighty fine artist," MoonKidd said, her small form soaring behind. *"We ain't even been in there that long and you already whipped up this sophisticated escape plan. Glad we got ye as friends."*

"Some friends you are," Nelsa replied.

She followed the guidance of her corpus through the maze of sewers. The tunnels shortly opened up into a larger hollow filled with lights and murmurs and bodies crawling in and out of elevated but poorly made shacks. The wet, slimy walls were covered in glowing defacements of Salazano and the Families. A low chorus of cheers spread from the houses as the sewer inhabitants noticed the passing fugitives. They always applauded anyone who went against the law.

"Oi, watch it!" a young kid dressed in rags yelled after Nelsa narrowly avoided flying into him.

The trio passed back into the narrow labyrinth of tunnels. They continued for another minute until Nelsa moved up a vertical tunnel and hit a dead end. Then she sent a hail. The black ceiling of this cylindrical shaft retracted and a violet mist quickly dispersed, sending a calm blue light down into the dim reek of the sewers.

"Up you come now," a familiar voice said. "Before those bloodthirsty lawkeeps catch your scent and doom us all."

CHAPTER ELEVEN

Reunited

"So, how've we all been, what's new?

MoonKidd lay with her legs up on the end of the lounge. She turned her head sideways and spat some baccy out onto the floor in a black muck, before looking back up at the ceiling, head bobbing away from her vigorous chewing.

A projection of the illuavan Jasolle coalesced into the room as though he were truly there. He growled, a deep droning sound and stared at MoonKidd with those large lidless eyes that flared with violent dark blues and reds.

"Truly remarkable that you would believe I'd welcome any scoundrel into one of my homes and allow them to spit upon my floor." The illuavan's voice was like the distant harsh whispers of a forest being crushed. "Do it again and I'll be inclined to spit a hole through your little head."

MoonKidd's eyes flashed with rage. "Did you just call me little?" she slowly growled. "You know I hate that, illuavan."

"Ah," Jasolle said. "So you do have ears! Perhaps it is

parts of your brain that you are missing. Thirty-eight times I've told you not to spit on my floors. And yet you continue to, every time I foolishly allow you back into one of my dwellings."

MoonKidd scoffed. "Seems you ain't got the wisdom to heed your own words, so why should I? The Jasolle who grew up in the dirt of the Frontier ain't never give a caosi about no baccy covered floor. You ain't even here anyways. Probably holed up in your fancy quarters ain't you? I'm sure you got a really nice view of old Sallyzano's tower."

"Everything I do is to help those like you. That includes putting on the guise of ally to the Families. I don't need your gratitude, but I certainly don't need your disrespect. I empathise with you StarFlower, I truly do." "She's just a bit upset," he said, slow and dazed. StarFlower sat beside MoonKidd on the lounge, smoking a thin cig and puffing out trails of green smoke. "On account of bein tortured and nearly killed. We're thankful, Jas."

"Well I ain't so sure we can trust this illuavan, Nel," MoonKidd continued. "Seems bein under the sway of the Families ismo for so long has changed him."

"Shut your caosin mouth," Nelsa snapped. "He just helped us escape the law and literally gave you the stala on your back. If you don't cut the messin around, I'll send you back to Belva mahself. Understood?"

"Easy, Nel," MoonKidd smirked. "Just havin a laugh."

Nelsa shook her head. "Thank you again for the place, Jas, and the stalas. You know we appreciate it,

MoonKidd especially."

"You know I will always do my best to help." The illuavans eyes returned to a calmer aqua.

MoonKidd scoffed, then her voice sweetened, if only a little. "Mars, how the black void are you? These last few months have felt like years, I swear."

Marston leant against a nearby wall with his arms crossed. "I've just been doin my thing. Few demolition jobs out west in the mines, few jobs in here, the occasional tendin out on the farms when I want to put my mind at ease. Same old, really."

"Keepin busy," MoonKidd said. "I like it."

"I see you ain't been stayin outta trouble. I'm glad to see you safe, Kidd. That goes for both of ye."

"I try to keep us out where I can," StarFlower said. "But you're all witness to my failins."

"Ease up." MoonKidd threw a hand back to slap him on the lap. "I'm the one that saved us from trouble when we first met."

"It's been ten years and you ain't never let that up."

Laughter rippled across the room.

"And I'm the one that came up with the idea of takin new names," StarFlower drawled. "Otherwise we'd all still be callin you—"

"Oi," she cried and slapped him harder this time. "You watch your tongue. You're lucky I named you after your soft demeanour and not your big head. Sorry, Nel. You went to all this effort to free us and we're talkin away. What's the target?"

"Wait a minute, Moon," StarFlower interjected. "Last

heist we did together didn't turn out so well. I'm not so sure we wanna get involved with you again, Nel."

Nelsa could see the cracked emerald veins in StarFlower's eyes from the compound drowning his brain in euphoria. Her stomach ached for some veroni. Seeing others indulging in their vices only heightened her anxious withdrawals.

She winced as the memory of her murdered family flashed before her eyes. A few bottles of veroni lay somewhere in Jasolle's house, but that would come later, along with all the ismo she could ever need to dull herself into oblivion. She shook herself. No. That's not why she was doing this anymore. She was doing it for herself. For the memory of her family.

"This is gonna be different," Nelsa said.

CHAPTER TWELVE

The Mark

"One of the other Families is helpin us," Maasi said. Zai floated beside Nelsa, gleaming and translucent with tendrils softly rippling below. "They've provided us with information. More importantly, an opportunity."

MoonKidd scoffed even louder this time. "How can you be sure it's one of them?"

"There ain't no one else it would be."

"And you're just gonna trust whoever this is?"

"We can trust that the other Families wanna see Salazano suffer and fall," Nelsa said. "He's been rulin for too long. This ain't the first time one o' the others has tried to take him down. The thing is, they've learnt to not be caught goin against him. They're lettin us do the dirty work. Whatever else they're plannin, well, it doesn't concern us."

"Take Salazano down?" StarFlower questioned. "You ain't serious? How are we supposed to do that exactly?"

"We're not," Nelsa corrected. "They're givin us an opportunity to deal a blow. We steal somethin precious to him, while fillin our minds with ismo."

"That sounds more doable. What's the mark?"

Nelsa accepted the hail from Maasi and her corpus took her consciousness away from her body. They floated in an artificial space between their minds. It was suddenly as though they stood upon the nothingness of the black void, looking at the planet Arkoma. Patches of orange, red and brown intersected all over the planet. One of its dual moons, Sanguul, sat to the side—unnaturally enhanced and like a sphere of congealed blood.

Thanks to their corpuses, their bodies remained suspended in the waking world while their minds existed here. They all stood next to one another, except MoonKidd, who still appeared to be laying down as though she floated around in the void still chewing baccy.

"The target is a long-lost heirloom precious to Salazano," Maasi said in zais multi-layered voice. "Beyond that we don't know. All that we do know is that he's bringin it all the way from the Velutra. I'm sure that our anonymous employer sees this as an opportunity to hurt Sal's pride—an embarrassment for his Family and rule if it is stolen. Where we come in."

Nelsa spoke and the surrounding realm zoomed in to display the immense black and gold fortress jutting out from the red moon. "The coscraft has already left the Velutra with the heirloom. It is scheduled to descend here in three days. The coscraft will first visit the Salazano fortress on Sanguul."

A vessel appeared from the dark reaches of the void upon a pale green river and then it swiftly made its way down to the fortress.

"Why stop at Sanguul?" MoonKidd questioned.

"Sal spends most of his time out there these days," Maasi answered. "Accordin to our information, he'll travel with it back down here to his tower. The coscraft will be heavily defended throughout the entire journey, so we'll need to hit them hard as soon as they land at the tower. Can't do it up there on the moon—we'd have nowhere to run or hide in the void."

"I didn't think of this before, Nelsa," Marston said, "but if our silent partner is just tryna hurt old Sallyzano, cain't we just destroy the cargo? Does it need to be stolen?"

"That ain't what we is bein paid to do," Nelsa said.

"Aight then," he conceded, twisting his curved hat. "But why the urgency?"

Nelsa glanced down into the nothingness, then back up. "That's the condition. We can't let the heirloom reach Salazano's tower. We don't get anythin otherwise. Besides, once it's locked up in his tower it'll be far harder to steal, if not plain impossible."

"So," MoonKidd said, spitting the baccy out into the nothingness. "Walk us through the details."

"We're thinkin o' doin a good ol smash-n-swap," Maasi said.

"Always an entertainin combo." MoonKidd's grin widened.

"Problem is, we don't exactly know what we're needin to replicate," Maasi continued. "We're gonna have to get someone into his Sanguul fortress and onto that craft in disguise. They'll see the object so our craft down on the planet can create the replica. We'll only have two minutes for that—the travel time from the moon to Sal's tower—and have it ready to swap at the interdiction point. That said, a couple chameleons fused together should be able to replicate whatever it is accurately enough to warrant no suspicion, at least till we get away."

"The short of it," Nelsa said, "is this: someone will be disguised in a chameleon right next to Salazano on the way down to Arkoma. They'll see the heirloom and deactivate the grav-sheath keeping it under lock. Then, just as it's about to reach the tower, we stir up a bit of chaos, and once we steal the original, we'll make em chase down the replica till we're in the clear."

MoonKidd pulled the lump of black baccy from her mouth and squished it repeatedly with her fingers. "You lot seem to be forgettin all the lawkeeps who will be glued to that thing and Salazano's side. Coscrafts patrollin the entire city, moon fortress and everywhere between. Not to mention those void eyes keepin watch from above and feedin anythin suspicious to the law. They've got that complete Velutran might goin against us. Now quit dodgin the question and tell me exactly how ye plan to do this swap."

Nelsa allowed a faint smile to grow on her hard face. Long before she got into duelling, stealing things was her way of life. She'd enjoyed it since childhood. At first it was just to survive the harsh Frontier, but it eventually grew into a skill she took pride in. Until she failed and her entire world bled into the sand.

This time would be different.

"Well," she said. "Marston's gonna blacken the cosmos."

CHAPTER THIRTEEN

The Plan

The mind space changed to display a coscraft landing inside the peak of Salazano's black and golden coiling tower. A mass of lawkeeps marched beside a glowing golden jewel twice their size whilst a dozen vessels lingered in the sky above as silent sentinels.

Marston took his hat off and ran a hand through his short and curly dark hair. "This jewel is just a placeholder till we know exactly what it is we stealin. Regardin the swappin, well, I had a deal that went awry a while back on account of a zenlian pack showin up. Mad-diseased abominations used a…well, me and my acquaintances decided to call it a Black Blinder. Watch."

One of the sentinel crafts fired a black bolt that devoured the jewel and the lawkeeps in a sphere of complete darkness stretching a short distance away from the tower.

"They use a harmless type o' modified nivlon energy," Marston continued, "but ye can't see nothin inside em. Perfect for doin business you ain't want anyone to see."

"Belva ain't got no eyes," MoonKidd said. "He sees through his corpus. Pretty much everyone in the Frontier has got one of those and can do the same if need be. I'm assumin at least one of us is gonna be in there and blind as well, so how're we gonna see?"

"The Blinder scrambles the corpus sensors as well as stalas. You're blind and quite disorientated, as though you're fallin forever into a Black Heart. It's not nice." Marston pushed his hat firmly back on. "We came up with a corpus alteration that mostly neutralises it. We won't be able to see with our eyes, but our corpuses will guide us through."

"Cosmic," MoonKidd beamed.

"How did you get this?" StarFlower griped, stepping closer towards Marston as though to throttle the smaller man. "Have you made a deal with the zenlians?"

"My business ain't any o' yours, friend."

"He's had a bad experience with that rotten lot," MoonKidd said with unusual sincerity. "Ease up, big flower. He ain't one o' them." She turned back to Marston. "How long does this blackout go on?"

"I got one that should be good for twenty seconds or so."

The darkness shrouding the tower and heirloom collapsed back to a singular point to reveal a conspicuously absent golden jewel. The coscraft that fired the Blinder raced away through the city in an attempt to get to the void and ascend away. In the simulation it was quickly surrounded by other lawkeep vessels, who dealt it targeted damage. Once its engines were shut off they captured it.

"Let me make an assumption," MoonKidd said. "That's the diversion with the replica."

They rapidly fell back through the planet's weak atmosphere and landed on another lawkeep craft that had remained behind to guard the tower. Its senyar hull suddenly became translucent, the gleaming golden heirloom hidden inside.

"As I suspected," MoonKidd said.

"At this point I'll detonate a whole heap of distractions at all the law coscrafts, as well as across the city, and we'll slip away in the mayhem."

MoonKidd grinned. "I can help you with those detonations, Mr. Devetta."

"That's Marston's expertise," Nelsa objected.

"Ahhh, c'mon," she pleaded. "I know a thing or two about distractions. I'm a wanted lass now."

"No."

MoonKidd spat. "What in the void do you have us doin then?"

"The only problem with this plan is that the roof of the tower needs to be kept open," Nelsa said. The simulation replayed. This time, as soon as the coscraft with the jewel descended into the large bowl at the tower's peak, the two coiling halves closed like two serpent mouths kissing. "We can't do the swap until the jewel is moved outside of the coscraft and into this open area inside the tower. Marston needs a clear line of sight above. So, someone has to enter the tower in disguise and take over the security room, re-opening the roof exactly at the right time. It takes ten seconds to open fully, but we ain't need that much time."

"And you want the both of us to do this?"

"That's right."

MoonKidd chewed for a moment. "We ain't no Slippery Belle. We ain't gonna be able to hit the security room quietly. Unless you got a few ideas?"

"As soon as Marston detonates the Blinder, we're gonna use a senyar drill and puncture a clean tunnel through the tower, at which point you'll have twenty seconds to get to the edge and into another craft that'll be waitin in the darkness."

"Wild."

"Why can't we just use the drill on the roof?" StarFlower said.

"Because it's infused with cryluss," Maasi said, "and won't be able to pierce it, as opposed to the senyar walls of the tower. The roof also has lumenshields protecting it which you will deactivate."

"I dunno bout this, Nel," MoonKidd said. "We only just got out of prison and you want us to go back into another. Bein right there in the heart of the tower, that might be the most dangerous spot in all the Frontier."

"And who is more capable?"

"Be nice."

Starflower pulled the cig from his mouth. "This seems more fittin for Maasi."

"The tower mechanics are wholly separate from their nexus," Maasi said. "Which I plan to hack beforehand. I can fabricate identities to get you inside, but on the day

I'll be keepin overwatch."

"If anythin goes wrong in there, as things oft do, then we're both as good as done," MoonKidd said.

"If it's any consolation you'll be heavily armed. But if you want the ismo then that's where you'll be."

"And where are you gonna get these two law co-scrafts?" StarFlower said, drawing hazy lines with the green smoke of his cig.

Jasolle spoke next. "You all know I make most of my wealth by purchasing used coscrafts out in Bazabarnia." The Four Families, including their Padrino—Malvatore Salazano—were indifferent to such ventures, so long as they were paid their taxes. "This commonly includes law crafts that I sharpen back into presentable shape. I have several that are operable, but we don't have the proper identity for them. That's where Maasi comes in."

"I'm goin to break into the lawkeep nexus to seize these identities," Maasi said. "Then I'll embed myself inside the nexus so I can keep up the guise and the supposed passengers inside. It'll take me a bit of time, but I'll get it done."

"Sounds solid."

"Hold up a minute," MoonKidd interrupted. "Me and the big flower are gonna be stormin this tower, but whose gonna be in the coscraft with ol Sal?"

"I am," Nelsa said. "I'll be disguised in a chameleon."

"Of who exactly?" StarFlower questioned.

"Salazano's nephew, Ciro," Maasi said.

The name sent a wave of scorching dread from her skull to her chest. She saw Ciro's eyes revelling at the blood spilt in the desert.

MoonKidd tugged at her braids. "Care to elaborate?"

"He's got a thing for a special kind of whore. One that we think will let Nelsa into his corpus so we can take control of him."

"So we're just gamblin that he'll take the bait? Our time's runnin out."

"He'll take it," Nelsa said.

"He always chooses a couple of hours before," Maasi continued. "Every day without fail. The identity we're makin should suit him perfectly. I'll come up with some other ideas if that doesn't work, but it's our best shot. Nelsa will board the coscraft on its journey from the moon. While there, she will send us a scan of the heirloom and release a program of my makin, corruptin their defences."

MoonKidd narrowed her eyes. "You said before that Salazano is gonna be on that coscraft. I ain't so sure that's the wisest idea puttin you by his side, Nel. Last I checked, he'd done you bad, real bad. No tellin what a hurt mind might do given such an opportunity."

"Good thing you ain't the wisest," Nelsa snapped back. "Nor did we ask for your opinion."

"Easy now." MoonKidd chuckled. "No need to be takin so much offence to my concern. This ain't no small thing. And you're speakin like we already said yes to our involvement. We haven't."

The artificial realm vanished and Nelsa returned to Jasolle's quarters. The others shifted and blinked as they re-entered their bodies. Nelsa marched over to

MoonKidd, who was still lying on the lounge. "You already forget how we saved your thick skin, salenai? You need only say you out and it'll be so."

"And here I was thinkin you'd done that outta the kindness of your vital."

Nelsa took a step back as MoonKidd finally sat upright on the lounge, her legs dangling just shy of the floor. "We're gonna need enough baccy and cigs to sustain me and precious here. Caosi, we're gonna need Costhrall on our side to pull this one off. Breakin us outta Belva's dungeon wasn't the first time you've saved my salenai skin. I'm with you, Nel. We good, ain't we big man?"

StarFlower dragged on his cig and nodded.

"Good," Nelsa said. Then she turned to the others. "Our roles are settled then. I'm goin up to Sanguul to get on the coscraft with the heirloom and Salazano. Jasolle and Maasi will be here keepin overwatch and feedin us everythin we need to know. Marston will fire the Blinder and pick up the heirloom and me. You two will get that roof open. Now, we've got lots of preparation to do, but we're gonna have to keep low these next couple days."

"Gonna be hard, on account of the bounties on our heads and all," MoonKidd said.

"We're gonna keep it low," Nelsa reiterated. "Any update on the chameleons, Jas?"

"They should arrive by tomorrow." Jasolle turned like a swaying tree towards the floating coavlen. "Maasi has already crafted a few identities for your needs."

"If they're comin from the Arnorath Covenant like you say then I'm sure they'll be of the highest quality."

"The chameleons are crucial to this plan succeed-in," Nelsa said. Then she turned to MoonKidd and StarFlower. "Especially in keepin you two from stirrin up any more trouble with the law. Until we get them, both of y'all will remain here." The salenai groaned again. "You ain't bein serious. I cain't be confined to these ghastly quarters. I get restless. And when I get restless? I. Get. Destructive."

Marston summoned a wanted sign with MoonKidd and StarFlower's faces side by side. Above them flashed the words: **Dead or Alive.**

"Big bounty on their heads now," he said. "We could just hand them over and reap the ismo." He gave the pair a wink.

Nelsa smirked. "Their heads ain't that big."

"Ha, ha," MoonKidd bitterly laughed. "Ain't none of y'all intellectuals yet to come up with an alternative to all this schemin. In my experience things don't often go accordin to plan."

"We still got three days to think on that before the heirloom arrives," Nelsa said. "But you're right. Fortunately we're known improvisers, just like when we bailed ye outta Belva's dungeon. Remember that?"

MoonKidd said nothing but gave a sly nod.

"All sorted then," Nelsa continued. "It's only a day. You'll be alright. We all have our own reasons as to why we need the ismo. But remember, it's Salazano we're goin against. He and his cursed family have scarred us all most of our lives. Now it's time for a little reparation."

CHAPTER FOURTEEN

Genocide of Genetics

Nelsa's weak hands pulled out the amber vial of veroni. A small part of her mind rationalised it. Deep down she knew she'd asked Jasolle for it just because she wanted to be numb, to forget about the heist and the grief that constantly gnawed away at her. The longer she went on, the harder it was to keep refusing. Nelsa slowly put the vial back inside a pocket in her stala.

"Well look at that," MoonKidd said after a scoff. "You could almost call it beautiful."

Out through the coscraft window, against the great darkness, a field of colourful scattered structures shimmered like a nursery of newborn stars. Each one had six long arms, splayed out from a central point like a child's drawing of a star. The bottom point, however, was twice as long. From the four points along the sides, smaller and upside-down versions of the same structures drooped off, as though the artificial star bore fruit. Even at a great distance the vats were immense in size.

The lights of many smaller crafts buzzed between each of the star-shaped vats. Some moved slower and were almost half the size of the vats themselves. All the ones she could see bore the crest of the Lecara Family. They held sovereignty over the mining and vat production of this region, so long as they paid their loyalty to Salazano with a constant flow of tributes.

"If only these vats were not owned by the Families," Starflower murmured. He and MoonKidd flanked Nelsa as he dragged. "Then the peoples of Arkoma would know prosperity."

"Perhaps," Nelsa said. "Perhaps they'd end up bein no better. Ain't sure true prosperity even exists. Even worlds in the Velutra fall to greedy hands like Salazanos."

MoonKidd gave Nelsa a side-eyed smirk. "Real optimist, ain't ye?"

"Somethin like that. Tell me, Kidd, do you ever think about goin to the Salenniun Kingdoms? Back to the home of your people?"

"My people?" MoonKidd scoffed. "They ain't my people. I ain't ever left the Frontier. I don't wanna go to the Velutra, Salenniun Kingdoms, or anywhere else. I may be a freak amongst outcasts here, but the Frontier is my home."

"You are not a freak," StarFlower said. "How many times do I need to tell you not to call yourself that?"

"Probably a few more."

"It is not your fault. Your ancestors were forced to evolve, as though you were some desolate planet for the worldsculptors to terraform. It was a genocide of genetics."

"Aye," she said. "We used to be humans just like y'all, and blah blah. But you don't know what it's like to be quite literally looked down upon by every other race. Even the cosless coavlens think we're freaks."

"You may be a freak," Nelsa said, "but not because of the colour of your skin or your stature. Your vital is the same as ours. We all just have different shells. I've only known a few salenais durin my time in the Frontier, but they've all had mighty strong vitals. They've been hardened with fortitude. That's somethin to be proud of, cuz I know for caosin sure you're one tough-to-kill, Malnetha-raisin scoundrel."

MoonKidd's grin glowed with mirth for a moment, then her expression grew unusually solemn. "You know, I ain't properly thank you for breakin us out, Nel. I know you didn't have to, but we appreciate it. Ain't no question that we owe you our lives. I know I can be a pain and all, but I—"

"As much as MoonKidd the Sincere is charmin," Nelsa interrupted. "I don't think I could ever get used to it. Ain't you hear all I just said? Why don't you just stick to bein MoonKidd the Obnoxious, the eternal pain in my vital." She flashed the salenai a sly grin and a wink.

MoonKidd beamed with delight and she started to bob about as though re-energised.

"I prefer the sincere you," StarFlower added.

"Sorry big man, the boss lady has spoken." MoonKidd chuckled and turned back to eye the field of vats. "All that senyar, cryluss and cryluns, ooooh. When we get done with all this, we should look into stealin one of these vats, whaddya reckon? Now that'd be a heist for history to remember."

Nelsa's smile grew. "I reckon you'd have to be a mad salenai named MoonKidd to pull somethin like that off. But I could see it happenin."

"Aye," MoonKidd said, reaching around to slap Nelsa on her backside. "There she is."

Nelsa raised her brows at the salenai but couldn't help the amused expression that crept onto her face.

Their coscraft continued past the collection of vats and then through a ringed security checkpoint for the outer regions. They were given clearance to travel on the pretence of sightseeing, as the wealthy often did. They weren't allowed in the vast asteroid belt that surrounded the inner planets—where the Four Families' precious resources awaited harvesting, though Salazano's domain even extended to nearby star realms. They only had permission to travel anywhere beyond the belt and their vessel propelled them forward at a tremendous speed through the asteroid field unharmed.

They shortly arrived at a smaller belt near the end of this star's territory. The coscraft marked their destination and the large black uneven shape of a solitary asteroid came into view. They flew to its dark surface, then inside a naturally hollowed out tunnel that would lead them to the meeting point at the heart of the cold rock.

"This is homely," MoonKidd chirped.

"You wanna get out of that tower alive?" Nelsa said. "Then we need this drill. Just be thankful I didn't keep you locked up in Jasolles. Now, activate your chameleons. We're here and you're both wanted. Can't have them becomin bounty collectors all of a sudden and tryin to claim you as a reward."

The black band around MoonKidd's neck disappeared and her entire body turned to a thousand crystallised shards of herself before they solidified like a rain shower from head to toe, changing her into a different person. Her height extended up to Nelsa's, her reddish skin paled and her muscles vanished. StarFlower and Nelsa's bodies changed in similar fashion, although into unremarkable identities Maasi created for them all.

"All good?" StarFlower asked. "Can't see the true me?"

"They're fine," Nelsa said, examining their new plain appearances. "We're good to go."

MoonKidd grinned. "They try anythin funny, Imma start blastin."

CHAPTER FIFTEEN

Negotiation

Nelsa descended down the coscraft ramp into the great cavern. MoonKidd and StarFlower followed, disguised in their chameleons. They walked towards the other vessel, its silver hull illuminating the entire hollow with its dull light. Two humans and an illuavan stood waiting.

Nelsa stopped a good distance from the dealers and kept her trembling hands hidden beneath her shawl. The chameleon disguise could only hide so much.

"Thanks for arrangin this on such short notice."

"It's the least I can do for our friend," Ospill said. He was a short, sturdy man—though not a salenai—and had black and grey unkempt hair.

"So, where's this drill?" As Nelsa asked the question, the drill drifted out of their coscraft and the dealers stepped out of the way to let it pass. It stopped right before her, a silver cone with no apparent features that was almost twice her height, though it was suspended off the ground. "A fine piece of equipment."

"Somethin ain't right," StarFlower said to her mind in

the joint channel.

"What is it?" Nelsa asked, continuing to walk around and pretend to inspect the drill.

"That man on the left, I recognise him. Black symbol on his neck. He's an outlaw. I know someone who had a run in with him just last year."

Nelsa accepted the hail containing the image StarFlower referred to. It was the same man, except he wielded a blade and was in the middle of thrusting it through someone's chest.

"So what? We knew Ospill would have brought protection. Can't be too picky out here."

"Fine indeed," Ospill said. "The drill will chew through ten metres of solid senyar in four seconds, easier than a crylun blade or anythin else. Hulls on the strongest Velutran crafts are not even that thick."

"And you've been makin these drills for the Families your whole life?" Nelsa was stalling now. She didn't care about his answer. Instead, she tried to focus on the rapid instant thoughts of the others in her mind, but the anxious dread stabbing her chest made it difficult.

"When the big man speaks you listen," MoonKidd said. *"These cretins mean to swindle us out of our coscraft and our lives. I told you we couldn't trust Jasolle."*

"My contact is solid," Jasolle said. He was back on Arkoma with Maasi and Marston, but distance didn't matter when speaking through a corpus. *"Ospill has a young daughter. If you really believe he's been compromised then they may have threatened her."*

"Maasi," Nelsa said. *"Get Ospill's address and see if you*

can hack anythin to check on his daughter. We can't reach out to Ospill's corpus and ask—if he's a hostage they'd have made him hand over control of his mind and body. And find out all you can about this outlaw. StarFlower, what about the illuavan?"

"I don't recognise them," StarFlower said. "I think Jasolle's right. They're usin Ospill to get a piece of our deal. The whole piece. I'd wager they've got a few other surprises inside that craft."

StarFlower and MoonKidd could be a nightmare to deal with, but Nelsa had learnt that when it came to shady deals and sniffing out intentions, they were a dream. She couldn't allow anyone she cared for to get killed. Not on her account. Not again.

"Aight, well, caosi. We ain't got the time for Maasi to confirm. How are we gonna do this?"

"Let's just take em," MoonKidd said.

"If that craft is secretly packin then they'll turn you to dust before you can yeehaw."

"I told you we shouldn't have come in that cruiser of Jasolle's. He had all those others in his private collection just sittin there."

"Shut up!" Nelsa snapped in their minds, her anger beneath the chameleon slightly leaking through her disguise. After years of use, most corpus users learn to keep the mind's emotions separated from the body's reactions when speaking through thought, but not everyone was going through withdrawals. All she had to do was take that vial out of her pocket and have a drink, then she'd be real calm.

"Enough about me," Ospill said, suddenly agitated. "The drill will meet your requirements. I've initiated the trade on an open hail. Accept so we can both be on our way."

Jasolle's voice came to their minds again. *"You even try to kill these outlaws, whoever is watching over his daughter is going to kill her without hesitation."*

"What are they waitin for if they mean to betray us?"

"What do you think, Nel?" MoonKidd said. *"They're waitin for that sweet ismo. Then they'll take the coscraft for their own."*

"Aight," Nelsa said. *"Until Maasi can confirm or they do otherwise, we negotiate without any killin. Jasolle, if we can't get out of it can we pay them off?"*

"I'm going to be wholly drained by the end of this ordeal, but yes. Negotiate with them. I do not want to see Ospill or his daughter harmed."

When she didn't answer for a few seconds, the human with the black symbol on his neck said, "Is there a problem?"

"Just a slight glitch," Nelsa said, turning away from the drill. MoonKidd and StarFlower repositioned themselves on either side of her and they all faced the three dealers. "You seem to think you can take advantage of us."

"What do you mean?" Ospill stammered.

"Before you do anythin rash like tryin to kill us, know that we can get you more ismo if you let him go alive." Nelsa slowly shifted her gaze from Ospill to the marked man, letting her eyes narrow in suspicion. She held it long enough to let him know that they were not fooling anyone.

The man blankly stared for a moment before a grin broke out. "How much more?" he said and then he put his arms around Ospill and gave him a shake. "Quite the valuable little man we got here. Not to mention his young one, just waitin to die should you not give us what we want."

"We'll give you double what we were gonna give you for the drill," Nelsa offered.

"Well that's very generous and all, but you see, we were plannin on commandeerin that coscraft behind you there. That alone has got to be at least worth four times this drill."

"Offer them the coscraft," Jasolle said. *"I can have another out to you in several hours."*

"Double for the drill and you can have the coscraft," Nelsa muttered. "But you bring the daughter here before you leave and then you'll get your ismo."

"Oh, I'm sorry," the outlaw said. "I hadn't finished listin our terms."

"Your greed is really startin to grind my vital," MoonKidd growled.

"You're still not considerin the value of this man's life. I know how much he's worth to me, but what are you willin to spend on him?"

"I would caution you not to overextend yourself," Nelsa said.

The outlaw formed a gun at Ospill's head who cowered but couldn't move. "Oh yea?"

MoonKidd and StarFlower had already drawn their rifles, but no one fired yet.

"Easy now," Nelsa said, putting her hands up and managing to keep them steady. She couldn't show any weakness, not now. "Everyone just remain calm. We can settle this reasonably without violence."

"Jasolle," she thought, *"does Ospill know who you are?"*

"No, only by the name HeartRot."

Nelsa matched the outlaw's mocking grin. "The one who organised this deal with Ospill in the first place is named HeartRot. You might not have heard that name before, but he's very well-placed under the Families. Particularly Salazano. It just so happens that he's listenin to our conversation right now and he's not likin what he's hearin. Not. One. Bit. So much so that he's already got three law coscrafts on their way right here."

Neck symbol scoffed. "You're just bluffin." Then he smiled and pressed the gun hard back into Ospill's head.

"He's got them in his pocket, so we'll be fine, but you…" Nelsa clicked her tongue and shook her head. "You kill us, they'll blow this entire rock to dust."

The outlaw turned his gun to Nelsa. "Then we'll just kill you and get out of here before they can come."

"By my estimates you have about three minutes to do that. Now that coscraft of ours ain't one that can ascend, is yours? Don't matter if it can, ain't gonna be anywhere you can hide in the Frontier where old Sallyzano won't hunt you down."

"I can't find the daughter," Maasi said. *"She isn't at their home in Scattertown. Maybe she's where the other outlaws*

are holed up—use that to keep threatenin him."

"I mean you can take your chances," Nelsa said. From her stala she projected a small screen for them to see. It was a live feed of their house in Scattertown from a watcher Maasi had hacked.

The outlaws gravely looked at each other and seemed to speak in thought. The illuavan's eyes flared as though two oceans were on fire.

Nelsa began to wrap up the negotiations. "You should probably know he's also got another four lawkeeps on their way there. If you're smart you wouldn't have kept the girl there, but if you're not, well…" She collapsed the projection screen. "We can still call them off. All you have to do is accept the original offer for the drill. That seems overly generous on our behalf, wouldn't you say? You get paid more than you deserve and everyone keeps their lives."

"You ain't gonna let us live!" he bellowed.

"Give us assurances for our lives," the illuavan growled.

Nelsa smiled. "What sort of assurance would you like?"

"Well done," MoonKidd said. *"But I would have rathered put a nice big hole through his head."*

"And that's why I'm in charge." Nelsa put her hands back in her shawl. Their jittering returned, but they found purchase on the vial of veroni and stilled.

CHAPTER SIXTEEN

Brighter Days Long Darkened

"Which one?" Nelsa asked.

A concoction of vulgar scents hung heavy in the air. A row of unconscious humans and illuavans lay on beds of black stone, as though she'd entered a morgue of fallen soldiers that awaited a farewell of being cast into a star. These bodies were not dead, however. Perhaps their vitals were emotionally dead like hers—that's why she was in a place like this.

"Second from the end," the serum vendor said. The frail old woman gave a wave of her hand that rattled with clunky jewels before hobbling out of the room. "Don't forget, you got an hour till I gotta wake em up."

Nelsa stalked through the silence. She was glad to be back on Arkoma after they settled the deal for the drill. This planet was her home. The reek of the room vanished as her stala masked her nose with clean desert air. She glanced to her right at a sanatare tree, and through the transparent silver bark, the pale green skin of an illuavan glowed in a meditative healing state. She continued on until she came to the second bed from the end. Its stone surface rippled with a deep blue mist as though a sentient ocean slumbered. Flowing with the undulating waves was a small sphere of colourful radiance—the coavlen's cryluss core: their lifeforce.

She'd never enjoyed such artificial enhancements to her cognition like this cheap serum of mimicry. Numbing herself with veroni was different. That's what she told herself.

"*Have you ever used rella like this coavlen?*" Nelsa thought to Maasi.

"*I ain't got no intention of returnin to Norella,*" Maasi replied from back in Jasolle's quarters.

"*No desire whatsoever? No longin for your homeworld?*"

"*Not in this false way. It ain't right,*" Maasi said. "*Besides, I made that sacrifice knowin the cost. The reason I left was more important.*"

"*You mean the human who you bonded with to venture to this wakin world? I ain't ever hear you speak of em.*"

"*And do I bring up your family's death outta the void? I don't think so. Just inject the coavlen so we can copy zais identity. We still got lots to do.*"

Nelsa pulled out a fine needle that Maasi had specially developed. With her other hand, she reached out and gently took the coavlen's core. Its warmth and vigour seeped into her flesh, as did the waking dreams of another realm, another life. In that moment all she knew were bitter regrets of a home that she could never return to.

The needle started to tremble with her hand as she held it against the core. Who was she to judge? She was no different to this coavlen seeking some vestige of better times, brighter days long darkened by the abyssal void of the universe.

The tight squeezing of her chest felt as though the claws of Malnetha twisted and scratched at her heart. The laughter of her children rang in her ears, the warm embrace of her love wrapped around her hands, but all her eyes could see was the blade stuck in each of their backs. All this, it was too much.

She needed to drink.

Resolved by her decision to down the veroni, Nelsa's hand steadied and she injected the needle into the coavlen's cryluss core. Its vibrant colours glowed brighter and shifted like liquid rainbows dancing on the surface of water. Slowly, she retracted the needle and with it, a vial of the coavlen's identity. She returned it to the protection of her stala to bring to Maasi. Yet she lingered for a moment, staring down at the cryluss core.

"Would you go back to Norella if you could?"

"It's impossible. It's the oath we take when we come here."

Nelsa peered deeper into the vulnerable orb of life. *"But if you could? Would you?"*

Even with the instant thought between their minds there was a delay before Maasi answered. *"No, this is the true world. It's where I wanna be, despite all its misfortunes."*

Nelsa scoffed. She was not so welcoming to the adversities of the physical world. Grief had a terrible hold on her. Strangely enough, this dull place of serum addicts made her feel like she was right at home. Lawkeeps

had burnt hers down the day her family died, but there
was a comfort in their shared addiction, their mutual
longing to return to better days.

Nelsa pulled out the small vial of veroni. She'd been
putting it off to remain alert and focused on the preparation required, but now she wanted a drink more than
almost anything. Almost as much as seeing her family
alive again. Malnetha itself could not stop her now.

Nelsa unsealed the vial and tossed the liquid down her
throat. It was good to be numb. Back home.

CHAPTER SEVENTEEN

Reasons

In a daze, Nelsa stared down at the dark ocean of blurred colourful lights. She often rode around on the grav-train in a stupor, watching the city fly by, and although she was in the middle of an operation, she had some time tonight.

Nelsa's chameleon disguised her as an inconspicuous nobody. There were so many faceless, disposable lives out in the Frontiers. Maasi had simply created another to fit in.

"I'm at the entrance," Maasi said to the joint channel. *"Five minutes to get in and out before they wake up. I can do this."*

Nelsa opened a window in her mind. With her waking eyes, she watched the coavlen enter a structure shaped like two crossed spires. It towered over most buildings in Arkoma City, the nexus of the Four Families. The Families stored any information they didn't want cluttering their minds in the nexus. A fortunate few permitted citizens drew upon the nexus for knowledge about the entire galaxy.

"*Remind me why I'm doin this again, Nel?*" Maasi doubted.

"*Ismo,*" Nelsa's dulled thoughts replied. "*Enough to...*"

"*To what? See me right for the rest o' my undyin life? I'm a coavlen, yet that does not mean I'm not without feelins. As you cosborn oft forget. What good is ismo, what good is livin, if all my friends are dead?*"

"*You've been alive for over three-hundred years, Maasi. You'll find new ones when we're all gone.*"

"*What a comfort you are, Nelsa Nolstar.*"

"*Why are you suddenly havin these doubts?*" Nelsa asked.

"*Maybe cuz I could die in here. Caosin fool.*"

Maasi now reflected the identity of the ever-shifting ocean blob from the serum den. As zai floated forward, waves formed and crashed upon the surrounding air. Maasi passed through the security checkpoint, confirming the false identity, and continued into a grav-sheath that lifted zai to the thirty-sixth floor.

A glowing humanoid form of shifting black and gold appeared before Maasi. When it spoke, a mouth formed out of bright lights. "Your prompt response to the attack on the nexus has been acknowledged. If you need any assistance, hail me." The stala guard collapsed into the floor like a rain of night littered with golden stars. Soon it vanished entirely, waiting elsewhere to be called upon.

Maasi said nothing and continued on as the entrance reeled open. The room itself constantly shifted around with countless tiny white spheres. A small river of misty water from Maasi's ocean form flowed into the glowing white spheres to physically access the nexus. Zai had fabricated the attack for this sole reason. While repairing the damage done and creating a defence against such future attacks, Maasi started to upload the program that granted zai access to the entire nexus of the Four Families and their coveted information. Undetectable and untraceable: Maasi's specialty.

"We're gonna have eyes all over the law," Maasi said. *"We'll see and hear everythin they do."*

"What if they find what you planted before we can even do this thing?" MoonKidd questioned from afar.

"They won't," Maasi said. *"Ain't my first time doin this. Besides, it don't even matter if the coavlen alerts them when zai wakes up. They won't be able to detect what I've planted, not in the next few days at least. They certainly won't be able to repair it by then."*

"Then how come you ain't already got eyes in there from before?"

"Cuz they're always updatin it. The last time I broke into it was from the relay in orbit around Sanguul years ago."

Two minutes passed before Maasi finished. The guard thanked Maasi on the way out and zai left out the front. *"Well that's a relief. Fleein outta here woulda been a real pain."*

"I woulda got you out with the Blinder," Marston said.

"Then we wouldn't have been able to do the heist."

"We woulda found another way," he said.

"I'm just glad I had at least one mind watchin over me."

Nelsa's corpus made it clear from Maasi's leaking

emotion that zais sarcastic comment was directed at her. The slightest twinge of guilt stabbed her chest. For a moment Nelsa thought she imagined it. She shouldn't have been able to feel anything. Not yet. The veroni Jasolle gave her must have been a bad batch.

"*So why are you doin this?*" Nelsa asked, not quite sure where the question surfaced from.

"*You were right, Nel,*" Maasi said. "*I need ismo to purchase cryluss so I can continue livin. What about you? Why are you really goin through with this?*"

Nelsa knew the reason. Doing this was the only way she could put an end to Salazano's tyranny. But Maasi couldn't know her true intentions. The coavlen may have been her best friend, but over the last years she'd purposefully distanced herself. She couldn't let another get close, only for them to get killed and tear open the already festering wound in her vital.

"*Ismo,*" Nelsa lied. "*Hoards of it.*"

"*The greed on your human tongue echoes a certain Family. And what are you gonna do with it? Numb yourself into oblivion? You need to get a caosin grip and cut off the veroni for good.*"

"*I can feel your thoughts leakin in again, Nel,*" StarFlower said.

"*You'll cost us this heist if you ain't get it under control,*" MoonKidd added.

"*We care about you, Nels,*" Marston said. "*We just want what's best for you.*"

"Quit your hollerin!" Nelsa screamed aloud and in thought. "I'll do whatever the caosi I want!"

Anger.

The veroni was definitely a bad batch. Nelsa cut her corpus off from the others.

Back in the grav-train cabin, she twitched around at the wide eyes of two people staring at her. Most of the other passengers paid her no attention, off somewhere in their own minds. Nelsa was still disguised but the two that looked at her now had certainly heard her shouting. Fearing that someone would call the law to arrest her, Nelsa connected to the train and casted herself down to the surface.

She landed in the middle of the street somewhere in Arkoma City where cheap and crumbling buildings still dominated the refined senyar towers. All around her flowed a dense mass of bodies. Anxious and trapped, Nelsa rushed towards the closest towers and along the sidewalk until she found a narrow alley to pass through. She didn't make it far down the lightless corridor until she collapsed to the hard grimy floor.

"I can't stop…" she wept. "I just want them back."

Her limbs were still numb, yet the dread in her chest burned worse than ever. A youthful, innocent voice cut through the fire of pain. A child calling for their mother.

Perhaps it was because she needed to punish herself. Perhaps it was because she just wanted to see her family again, no matter the circumstances. Or perhaps it was because she needed the courage to keep going, to finally give up the veroni and face Salazano, but Nelsa knew what she had to do next.

She crawled over and rested against the wall. A pro-

jection screen appeared and she dazedly stared at the
rectangle as shifting colours started to form. Then Nelsa
called forth the most painful memory of her life. The file
in her corpus titled:

Salazano sends his regards.

CHAPTER EIGHTEEN

Blood in the Sand

Purple blood from the mutilated steed stained the sand. A mixture of low quality Frontier mechanical and biological engineering, gutted for the world to see. Nelsa's family had often ridden the creatures out here in the desert wasteland. She wasn't there for their final ride.

A man stood near the corpse, giving his everything to protect the two small children clinging to his legs. Their father fiercely swung his blade to keep the encircling assassins back.

"Stay back!" he cried. "I'll kill whoever takes the next step! Stay back!"

The assassins ignored his threats, playfully swaying with each step, laughter rippling between them. The black of their attire stood stark against the ashen brown landscape, while the golden half blended deceptively into the shimmering sands.

Behind the enclosing killers, towering upon a ragged boulder, stood The Hand of Chaos. He wore a golden vest with several dark embroidered patterns, cloaked in a long dark coat, darkness seeping from its edges. Unlike most in the Frontier, he had no hat. His dark hair was short and smoothly slicked back, set with several golden lines of glittering gems. They matched his earrings, a golden planet pierced by a blade. The Sal Family crest. His left hand was dressed in a gold and black glove. The other was exposed and only had two fingers and one thumb, all of which were deformed and covered with black etchings of strange symbols. Dark hollows that used to hold his eyes stared out of his gaunt and pale face. He grinned as his personal band of assassins slowly closed in.

Three coscrafts circled low in the air like scavengers waiting to feed on carrion. They recorded the scene for Nelsa, continually changing angles as though she watched some kind of depraved dramatised reenactment. Everything was the way Salazano had wanted it. He wanted Nelsa to watch them struggle. To see their growing desperation. Their slow death.

Nelsa caught the wet glimmer of despair in Teec's eyes. It was the realisation that he was going to die. All his hopeful dreams of the future would soon be lost to the cold void. That he was a failure. Then she saw that despair descend into a dark resolve.

Teec's blade moved down towards the children. He would give them the quick and merciful death that Salazano would surely deprive them of. But he was immediately waylaid. Black whips wrangled around each of his limbs and he cried out in anguish, their bite digging into his bleeding skin and forcing him prone into the sand.

The children were torn away by more shadowy whips that wrangled around them into the sand with their small heads bent back to look at their father. Their tears watered the lifeless desert.

Both of the children screamed the air out of their lungs, lost in the hysteria of pain and fear. But through the wailing Colquin eventually shouted, "Dada, why are they doing this?"

"Close your eyes, son!" Teec bellowed.

The assassins' black whips crept, like pulsating tentacles, pried their clenched eyes open. An assassin stood at the feet of each children and Teec. The three killers held the whips in both hands like tight chains. Belva walked forward until he stood towering over Kayli, an eyeless apparition spawned from the nightmares of Malnetha. A black starrise.

"Transgressions must be repaid," Belva hissed. He formed a quivering, hungry blade.

"I want Mama," Kayli wept. Her blue eyes rattled with terrified shock.

"Hey, hey, hey," Teec stammered, trying to comfort his daughter through Belva's legs. "It's all gonna be alright. Remember that story about the river and a place called the Cos Realm? Yea, focus on that. We're gonna go there."

"What about Mama?" Colquin sobbed.

"She's gonna join us later. Don't worry about that."

"I'm scared Dada," Kayli whimpered. "What if Mama—"

Belva's blade crunched into her bone and flesh. He

twisted it around as Kayli's convulsing body slowed and her gurgling breaths sputtered out blood. Then silence.

Nelsa broke all over again. Her daughter's choking rasps raged through her mind like the burning tidal wave of a dead star. Nelsa forgot she was cowering in that dark alley. It was as though she were really there, the warm sand rough against her skin, her tears diluting the blood of her murdered child, the desert wind muddled with the laughing assassins.

Belva pulled the blade from Kayli with a wet woosh and his boots crunched against the desert as he stepped over to Colquin. Sand littered his curly brown hair and stuck to his face. His small arms and legs thrashed against the writhing black strands that pinned him down. The bawling young boy now crumbled into shocked whimpers, but they cut off as Belva stuck his blade through Colquin's neck.

Teec thrashed in a blind rage but they kept him pinned down. He broke. Belva let Teec writhe for a few moments longer before he thrust his blade into his back. Teec gasped and sputtered, but he still had some strength—he lifted his head and spat blood on Belva's boots. Then he fell limp into the sand.

The recording ended and the projection screen went black and then returned to her stala.

"Salazano sends his regards."

The bloody words attached to the hail crashed back into her mind where they had festered for years, dripping their torment into every waking thought. The numbing effects of veroni were the only thing that had ever silenced them. Not even that could protect her now.

CHAPTER NINETEEN

Change

Cradling herself in the dark alley, Nelsa's heavy breathing turned into wheezing, aching sobs. She lay like a wounded creature on its deathbed. There she wept. For her family. For herself. All the pent-up sorrow gushed out in a flood of tears that could have swept the city away.

Through her blurry vision her eyes still saw the sands where they died. She returned there once, years later. She laid where they died, about to kill herself. But in that moment her anger kept her alive. That had waned over the years as her quest for vengeance failed and sorrow took over.

Nelsa hadn't been there for her family. She kept no token of them save for the scar in her mind. No precious item to weep over except for the gaping hole in her vital that no amount of tears could seal. They had been reduced to nothing but bloody stains in the desert, blown away by the sandy winds.

"No," she said, wiping away the gushing tears. "They will always be my children. My beautiful children. My

Teec. My love."

The hopeful thought met the shuddering sickness of the vile veroni crawling through her veins. Then her vital snapped. She would not endure it for a second longer. Nelsa rummaged through her stala and pulled out a miniscule capsule of a sobriety serum that she'd stored for years. She'd felt nothing about lying to Maasi at the time, but now she felt guilty for all the lies she'd told. Yet there was one lie she still had to keep.

Nelsa injected it into her veins. She shivered from the cold rush and exhaled a deep groan as she truly came back into herself. In that moment it felt as though her body had thawed from drifting in the cold void. Nelsa fell back against the wall and closed her eyes, trying to control her heavy breathing as time slipped away.

"This brings me back," a rustling voice said.

Nelsa's eyes shot open. Jasolle leaned against the dark corridor.

"I used to hide away in alleys like this all the time," the illuavan continued. "Long before I figured out how to survive and thrive, I would sit in the quiet dark and take my mind away to the great Kals Gasirei of my kind. I still come back to remind myself of where I came from so I don't get lost in the Families' corrupting splendour."

"Why don't you abandon that fake life altogether?" Nelsa said, exhausted.

Jasolle turned to face her. His skin and fine robes were dark shades of green, but his lidless eyes gleamed like two dull white orbs. "And what? Flee and hide away in luxury and comfort until the lulstolo calls me to the above? My purpose is here on Arkoma. I do good, more so than I would be able to elsewhere. You don't think you're the only ones I help, do you?"

"No," Nelsa said, then she shot him a weary smile. "But we're your favourite group of thieves right?"

"Oh, I don't know about that," he rustled. "You and your friends have certainly cost me the most. But there is no limit on the ismo I'm willing to spend to keep those I care for alive and well. Thank you again for how you handled the deal. Ospill and his daughter are grateful."

"Let's just hope those outlaws keep their word and don't ever come back this way."

"I believe you scared them enough."

Nelsa looked away and then down at her thumb as it rubbed against her palm. "You put somethin else in the veroni you gave me, didn't you?"

"You truly think I would intentionally assist in your addiction after all this time? Nelsa, you're more out of touch than I believed."

She stopped and stared up at him. "What do you mean? What did you give me?"

"A drop of Elanion. It is said to form a strong passage for the conscious mind to the vital, to the self. Did you feel something peculiar?"

"What gave you the impression that I required such a thing?"

"Oh, just my illuavan intuition. Am I wrong?"

Nelsa glowered and turned away, then her expression broke. "Now I can't tell if it was that or my own volition which made me flush the veroni away."

"You do realise that this isn't the first time you've got veroni off me? I've given you Elanion before. It only works when the vital decides it's ready for change. You accepted you were ready for change, ready to stop running from grief."

Jasolle walked over and held out his long slender hand. "I'll fix you up something for the withdrawals back at my place. Always endure. Always forward."

Nelsa stared at his hand. There was a strange aftertaste of the sobriety serum that she wasn't accustomed to, some kind of sorrowful rejuvenation. Or perhaps it was from the Elanion.

"You might not have seen it because of all this," Jasolle breezed. "But Ciro took the bait. Come on now, we don't have long until we begin. They're all counting on you."

Nelsa swallowed, then she drew a deep breath and reached out. It would take her a moment to find her footing. She didn't care about getting up on her own as long as she got back up.

CHAPTER TWENTY

Bitter Reciprocation

Nelsa sat on a lounge in a dark room, hands cradling her head. She'd been here on her lonesome for two hours now. Jasolle had fixed her up with a hot tea that soothed the already rising craving. All that was left now was for Maasi to finish tinkering with the chameleon she would use to get up to Sanguul and begin the heist.

She rubbed her eyes and pulled her hands away. She looked down at her lap and lifted up the solid orb that lay there. It was small enough to hold in the palm of one hand and its exterior shifted with blood-red currents.

"What're ya lookin at?" A voice like a stiff rumble of thunder entered the room.

Nelsa blinked. Startled, she closed her fingers around the sphere and quickly placed it against her chest. Her clothes rippled with violet mist and absorbed the sphere, keeping it hidden.

"Oh," she said, clearing her throat and trying to remain calm. "Nothin. Just…just somethin I've been holdin onto for a long time. What can I do for you, Mars?"

Marston leant against the doorway. "We never settled on the volume of said distractions." He tilted his hat back to display those stern dark blue eyes. "How much of this city am I allowed to destroy?"

Most only ever saw a coldness in his eyes, but beyond that calloused exterior she'd always seen a sensitive ocean of compassion. She'd felt him extend that rare kindness of his to her before, but she could never reciprocate the way he wanted.

"Loud enough so that the Sages all the way over in the Velutra can hear."

"Aye," Marston said, smiling beneath his thick brown moustache. "So pretty loud. Old Sallyzano won't know what hit him."

"Just don't wipe out the entire galaxy, aight?" Nelsa said, mirroring his faint smile. "No killin, not even the law, aight? We can't have innocents dyin on our account."

"Just who do you think I is? I ain't no villain."

"That's what every villain says."

They looked at each other hard before they both broke and chuckled. Then she watched his smile fade the longer they continued to look into one another's eyes. He finally broke contact and looked nervously around before he cleared his throat and brushed his moustache.

"Now I remember the real reason I came to see you." Marston walked over and held open his hand. From the bottom of his sleeves a blue mist drifted down onto his palm and coalesced into a small misty cylinder tapered to a sharp point. "This here's a stala-piercin bolt o' cryluns.

It's only enough for one shot, but it's just in case."

"A stala…bullet," Nelsa stammered. "But how did…"

"They ain't cheap, but I—"

"Ain't cheap? Mars, this…this is worth at least twice the amount we're gettin paid for the heist."

"I know, I know. But I didn't pay for it. Came into my possession the same time as I got the Blinder, if you recall."

She couldn't help but think of selling it and abandoning this heist. It'd be enough for her to get numb for the rest of her miserable life. But that wouldn't hurt Salazano. That wouldn't get her the vengeance she craved.

"You ain't dealt with those zenlians since then, have you?"

"Course not, have you?"

Nelsa cast her eyes down for a moment, then back up. "You've had it for that long?"

"I ain't had the need to use it, nor could I ever bring myself to sell it. I ain't care that much for ismo anyway, just need enough to get by. So I figured…"

"You figured what?"

"You'll have a moment in the Blinder to put this in old Sallyzano's skull. Right at that last moment before I lift you up, you do it."

"Mars…I can't take it. You keep it."

"It's yours, Nels," he said. "It belongs to you. Put it to good use."

Nelsa knew she wouldn't be able to refuse his offer. She reached out and touched the bullet and her stala carried it away to safety. "Just in case," she said. "Thank you, Mars." Her hand remained there and it gently fell down upon his. For a moment they shared that deep look they'd shared before, until Marston pulled away and took a step back.

"Well, I got lots to do," he said, tilting his hat back down. "Cain't afford to be chattin away with pretty ladies all day."

He turned to leave but Nelsa called him back. "I'm sorry, Mars." Her voice was fragile, like a star teetering on the edge of a Black Heart. "Sorry that I could never reciprocate what you felt between us. I...I'm too far g—"

"You ain't ever gotta be sorry or explain yerself," Marston interrupted. "It's just like I told you back then: I ain't ever gonna be able to properly understand what you've been through, but I'll always be here with a helpin hand for when you stumble." "I just...I hope you ain't been stickin around cuz of me."

Marston gave a short laugh. "You sure is pretty lookin and all, but no. I ain't been lingerin in this degradin city just for the chance you'll heal all your sorrows and change your mind and fall in love with a fool like me."

"Then why?" she asked, a tinge of desperation in her voice. "You could be away from all this and out there doin greater, better things. But no, you stay here in this forsaken city, suffocated by these forsaken sands, watchin over me wherever I go. Or did you really think I haven't noticed after all this time?"

Marston swallowed. Those hard blue eyes softened. "You're one of the only ones to treat me right, Nels. And

I'll always love you for that, in more ways than one. I'll admit that some dark part of me wished every time you left my sight and went down to duel that you wouldn't come back up. That your sufferin would finally end. Yet each time you stepped back out into the bright lights, relief would wash over me like rain over those lifeless plains. I ain't got no children to love or mourn, if you'll forgive me sayin so. I ain't got no friends save you, Nel. Void, maybe I am stayin around for your sweet smile, but that's my choice, one I own completely. You ain't gonna be able to say nothin to sway me otherwise."

A storm of feelings raged around inside her now. Love. Sorrow. Guilt. Regret. She started to speak, unsure what to say, but compelled to at least say something. No words came out. She just sat there silently gazing at him, trying to think of ways to express how she truly felt.

"It sorely pains me to see how you're hurtin yourself every day," Marston continued. "I never thought it was my place to say anythin, but I guess considerin how I think of you as a true friend and all, well, allow me just to say: you've been grievin for far too long without grievin, if you understand my words. You ain't ever gonna heal your vital if you keep hidin from it. You've been disrespectin the dead, Nels. It's time you find the courage and give them the honour they deserve. It's time you get your retribution and be done with it for good."

Nelsa watched him tip his hat and turn to leave.

"Mars…" she softly called out. But this time she couldn't call him back.

CHAPTER TWENTY-ONE

The Painful Bite of Clarity

In the devastating absence of Marston, Nelsa sat in her darkening unease. The pressure of this operation had started to brew like the raging dust storms beyond the city outskirts, but now it intensified into disorientation and dread.

Nelsa wasn't worried about her own life. She had forsaken it long ago. Now she had brought her friends into peril and would take them further into harm's way. The weight of that responsibility settled on her shoulders. Despite their yearning for ismo, they counted on her. Believed in her. She questioned whether she was doing them wrong, yet every thought returned to Salazano. This had to be done.

Maasi drifted into the room, filling it with the jelly-like coavlen's pale blue aura.

"We're all set," Maasi said. "The two law coscrafts are prepared. Marston's Blinder is installed and ready to blacken the city. MoonKidd and StarFlower are waitin to go into the Tower on your command. Drill is ready in the other coscraft for their extraction. And you're ready to become a first-class Frontier courtesan. All the information of your new personality and life are embedded within the chameleon. Need only absorb it and you'll be right for any questionin down here and up on Sanguul."

One of zais tentacles held out a thin black band and passed it to Nelsa. "Grav-train departs in two hours. You gonna be ready? Only got one shot at this, Nel. No shame backin out now if you ain't fully committed."

Nelsa's eyes fell to the floor. "I'm good."

"You could convince a star of being a Black Heart with that tone," Maasi said. "What dark thoughts have your mind in a bind? Speak em now."

She slowly lifted her head to face the coavlen, but couldn't find any words. She looked away.

"Come on, out with it. Keepin things all locked up inside doesn't do anyone any good. Especially not before a heist. It's bad luck, so spit it out."

Nelsa bit her tongue for a moment then let go. "It's just every Costhrall forsaken thing, Maasi. It's this entire mad Frontier. It's never bein able to go back. To truly right wrongs. It's knowin the scum controllin this city still draws breath." Nelsa's head sunk lower. "It's livin without them. It's tryin to hold onto the courage to do what I need to, but it just keeps on slippin away."

Maasi drifted closer, zais tendrils rippling with tender melancholy. "Ain't no words o' mine gonna be able to lift your vital outta this despair, Nelsa. Gotta do that yourself, but only if you truly want. I'm here for ya, friend. We're gonna hurt the villain the only way we know how. Take what he holds dearest. All I need to hear is that you're gonna be good. You ain't the only one puttin themselves in harm's way."

"I'm good," Nelsa muttered, eyes still fixated on the floor and hidden by her hands cradling her head.

"Mind repeatin that?"

Nelsa exhaled a deep breath and looked up to face the glowing coavlen. "I'm good, Maasi," she said, her voice and eyes firm with resolve.

There was a long pause. "Marvellous." Maasi wasted no time in drifting out of the room. "Grav-train departs in two hours. I'll give you some more time to yourself, then we'll meet to go over the plan one last time. I expect you to shed this broodin aura by then." With that, Maasi left Nelsa alone again.

Nelsa spun around on the lounge and laid down, staring up at a ceiling that projected the night sky. The stars were serene in their distant quietude. They sang to her sober eyes of a comfort she had once known. In their dim magnificence, she wondered how many others across the galaxy were contemplating a life better than their current one under Malnetha's rule.

She thought back to the time her family laid in the desert looking up at the same night sky. Colquin had asked what was out there and Teec answered. Kayli sang and they hushed, listening. Teec told a joke that everyone thought was terrible but they all laughed anyway. They fell asleep there and woke up huddled together under the warm beams of light from the starrise.

An unwanted desire to be numb made her stomach heave. These were beautiful, cherished moments and she would no longer hide from them. As though Arkoma's Star shone on her again, warmth and vigour coursed through her veins. Determination numbed her sorrow.

"I'm doin this for them," she said, squeezing both her fists. "There can be no turnin back."

CHAPTER TWENTY-TWO

Revelry

Nelsa was the only whore not smiling.

With her chameleon projecting her courtesan disguise, Nelsa sat by her lonesome at the bar, fiddling with a glass and continually eyeing the entrance. Her target would walk through any moment.

The other courtesans that had been ferried up to Sanguul Fortress—both men and women, illuavans, coavlens and even a warlif—entertained their patrons. Scattered across this room filled with lounges, golden statues, and dim orbs of suspended light, everyone indulged in drinking, injecting, smoking, laughing, and fondling one another.

Every night Salazano's gold guards—whoever was not on duty—descended into debauchery. It mattered not that in a few hours they would be tasked with guarding the heirloom down to the planet. It only took a second to flush a mind and body sober. Nelsa knew that better than most.

A woman adorned in the black and gold robes of an off-duty guard plopped herself down beside Nelsa.

"Light of Costhrall guides me," she mumbled. The re-fined Velutran manner still clung to the woman despite her inebriation. "Your beauty has smote my vital. What a delicious thing you are. Where have you been hiding all these years?"

Nelsa's current identity was of Carain Naoff. A new-comer to this region of the Frontiers, but a courtesan whose renown, beauty, and specialities had been falsely spread by Maasi to specifically attract one high ranking gold guard.

"At least I know my disguises are gettin better," Maasi said in thought. The coavlen waited in Jasolle's quarters down on the planet where zai watched every aspect of the operation. *"A whore? Bounty collectors? Lawkeep? A distant noble? Step right up to Maasi's Makeovers and I'll make you whoever you dream of."*

"Shame you can't wear it permanently, aye Nelsa?" MoonKidd added. *"Ah, wish I was the one up there. I could teach them all a thing or two about pleasurin flesh."*

"Afraid I'm already taken for the evenin," Nelsa said, ignoring the thoughts in her mind. "I'm sure one o' these other fine ladies can satisfy your needs." This guard couldn't help her infiltrate the vessel with the heirloom and Salazano.

"The unrefined mouths on you Frontier whores…I have such a love-hate relationship with them." The woman chuckled. "And may you permit me the knowl-edge of who has acquired you for this evening's enter-tainment?"

Looking past the intoxicated gold guard, she saw the

man she had come for. It was fortunate she wore her chameleon disguise, because her true expression was one of seething rage. Ciro Salazano, nephew of the Padrino himself. Not only was he present at her family's death, but he'd held Kayli down while Belva murdered her. It took everything for her not to push the woman out of the way and put Marston's bullet in his skull.

"Remember," Maasi said. *"We need him alive. Don't lose control."*

"I got it, Maasi," Nelsa replied. She gestured for the pestering guard to look behind and when she slowly turned around to see, the woman scoffed and stumbled away. Nelsa remained fixated on the man. Ciro wore no expression except for the permanent scowl on his brutish face. When his narrow dark eyes locked onto hers, he turned and left, but a hail came to her mind, beckoning her to follow. She was the whore he had paid for. There was no need for flirtatious introductions.

Nelsa released her tight grip around the glass. She regained her composure, pushed herself off the chair and started to leave, but on her way out the same woman called out, "Be a good whore now! Don't be too rough or he'll cast you into the cold with all the others!"

A burst of laughter scratched across the room. Nelsa didn't spare any of them a glance, but their snickering echoed in her mind as she left.

Nelsa followed Ciro at a distance through the grand hallways of polished black stone in Salazano's Sanguul keep. Floating golden braziers lit the passage-ways, bathing the golden statues with brilliance. Visible through tall windows of clear glass, the planet silently hung in the void like a drifting red marble. Nelsa stopped at one and marked the patch of light that was Arkoma City. Her home.

"Why'd they have to come out here to the Frontiers?" she said to no one in particular. *"Why couldn't they just be content in the Velutra?"*

"They don't got power over others like they do here," Maasi answered. *"They had to conform to the Sages and their Virtues and laws. Out here they is the Sages, they is the law."*

She blinked away visions of bloodied sands and realised Ciro was no longer in view. That didn't matter—she had the directions in her mind. She continued on.

She reached an arched doorway in the black stone. It dissolved into a golden mist that veiled what lay beyond. She pushed through. The room reeked of Velutran refinery with its fabricated odour, elegant yet simple in its furnishings, finely carved golden statues, and gleaming jewels that hung from the ceiling. Ciro was already in a chair by a tall arched window looking out into the starry void. Through nothing more than a harsh stare, he invited her to be seated in the empty chair directly opposite him.

Nelsa obliged.

Jasolle's rustling voice came to her mind. *"Revenge is best delivered cold, like the void."*

"Thanks for the philosophy," Nelsa replied in thought. She stared straight at Ciro in their brooding silence. *"Not*

really feelin it right now."

"*Why do you think I said it?*" Jasolle answered.

Once she took her seat, Nelsa crossed her exposed legs and leaned calmly into the backrest. She pulled out a thin cig from the bosom of her velvet green dress and placed it into her mouth. She took a long slow inhale before pulling it out and blowing an arrow of smoke straight across into Ciro's forehead. It rolled back into his short black hair.

"So," she said. "You've brought me here to play some games. Let's begin, shall we?"

CHAPTER TWENTY-THREE

Courtesan of the Moon

"We will begin when I say so," Ciro said, voice rough and accusatory. "Why did you leave Bazabarnia?"

"You lot sure like small talk, don't ya?" Nelsa said with a thin grin. "I thought I was brought here to satisfy?"

"You'll satisfy me by doing whatever I say, which right now is answering my questions."

Nelsa unfolded her legs and crossed them the other way. It took everything not to leap across and slit the man's throat, not that she'd succeed. Marston's bullet could though. No, she needed that for Salazano just in case. The precious red orb hidden beneath her chameleon burned against her chest. Everything relied on that.

She had her chameleon for the disguise, but she didn't have her stala here. She would not have made it past the security check—no such Frontier courtesan would possess a full stala. Even if she had it here, there would be no fighting this man. He was a gold guard and would kill her with devastating swiftness. She had to defeat him with deception.

Nelsa clicked her tongue. "Ah, so that's why you asked after me. You're harsh upon the world and its inhabitants, and you like to be pleasured accordingly."

"I will not warn you again, whore. My question. Answer it."

"I left Bazabarnia because I grew sick of the sycophants and borin clients. I wanted to find more…sharpened horizons." Nelsa spun the cig around her fingers before it landed back in her mouth. "Remains to be seen if I found the right world."

"When did you first indulge in the pleasures of flesh?"

"Twenty-four. I bloomed late." Nelsa winked.

"How many times have you dominated?"

"Corpus, crylun, my own hands? I have many talents. You'll have to be specific, darlin."

"Crylun."

Nelsa chuckled. "Well I'm pushin one-hundred and twenty now, so, precisely 23,128 separate times. But you already knew that from absorbing my provided history. Again, you former Velutrans sure do like chattin away. I'm assumin this is a little routine of yours? Try to get some vestige of control before the humiliation sinks in?"

Ciro sternly eyed her in silence until he said, "You're to do exactly what is instructed in the hail I sent you. If there is one false move…" A mist drifted off his robes and stopped behind Nelsa, where it solidified into a gleaming black blade. The sharp end pointed right at the back of her neck. "You're done."

Nelsa firmed her vital as hard as senyar and continued

speaking. "I'm afraid that's not gonna fly, sweetness. You've seen my history, and you know I ain't no ordinary crylun dominator. Any regular courtesan can do what you want. You asked for me specifically because of the special services I offer. Because of what I picked up in the pleasure dens out Bazabarni way. Grant me control o' your corpus and I'll pleasure your mind in ways you never dreamed of."

"Don't be a fool, whore."

She licked her lips. "So vulgar. Don't you know we prefer the term courtesan?"

"Just shut your mouth and do as you're told."

"Oh." Nelsa giggled. "So feisty. I ain't the fool that's never been at the mercy of a corpus dominatrix. You have nothin to fear, sweetness, it's safe. You need not hand over control of your entire corpus—that would indeed be foolish. You'll see from the hail what I need to satisfy you like you ain't ever been before. Go on. See for yourself."

"You'll be a dead fool if you don't silence your tongue."

Nelsa's playful expression vanished and she became cold. "If you want to stick to this child's play, by all means. I couldn't care less as long as I get paid. Though I'd be remiss not to try and earn a generous tip by unlocking new desires that'll leave you feeling like Costhrall itself descended to pleasure ya."

Nelsa uncrossed her legs again, though this time she slowly stood and took a step forward before leaning down to look into his curious, lustful eyes. She placed a gentle hand on his thigh. As she continued talking her hand climbed up and pressed firmly down. "Or perhaps more to your likin, it'll be like Malnetha descended to rule over you. What I want to know, pathetic man, is when are you goin to let me into your corpus so I can teach you how worthless you are."

Ciro's harsh countenance returned for a long moment, so long that Nelsa thought he might just kill her right there. Then he swallowed. She had him. "Teach me, please." He trembled, averting his gaze. Nelsa felt the hail from his corpus, along with a small mist of the man's cryluns.

"That's a good little pet," Nelsa said. "Don't you look at me again unless I say so."

"*Holy void*," MoonKidd said in thought. "*You've got me goin! I'll be savin this memory for later.*"

"*Cut it out, you deviant!*" Maasi said. "*She needs to focus!*"

Nelsa stepped back to her chair, sat down, and continued dragging on her cig. Now granted access into a tiny fragment of his corpus, Nelsa immediately uploaded the program Maasi had developed to take complete control. Like water being poured over sand, it seeped into the security defences.

"*It's workin,*" Maasi said, "*but it'll take a minute to finish. Keep his mind and body distracted the best you can to minimise the chance of him noticin.*"

Commanding the mist of Ciro's cryluns, Nelsa forced the small violet cloud in through his ears. From there she eased into her role as a crylun dominatrix. As the minute organic machines drifted down beneath his flesh they danced upon his muscles, played with his veins, tickled the inside of his skin, and scratched his bones with painful delight.

"Now," Nelsa said. "I am a professional, and as such, safety comes first. If at any point you want our activities to stop, then think about a red flower growin out of a desert."

Ciro's eyes fluttered in pleasure and looked across the chair to Nelsa.

"What did I say about lookin at me!" she yelled, and scratched his bones harder, causing him to shudder.

Then, even though he had his eyes closed and was looking away, she gave him a lewd lick of her lips and continued. "More of a safety precaution for me in case I get carried away."

"Yes…mistress," Ciro stuttered.

"I'll tell you how worthless you really are." Nelsa spat across the chairs and it landed directly on his face, which he allowed to pass through.

He was still in control of his stala. His tongue poked out and licked the saliva dripping down into his mouth.

"You're the scum that grows in dank places void of light. A grain of insignificant sand amongst the desert. You're the shadow of greatness that never amounted to anythin. Pathetic. You had everythin handed to you by your family and yet you still managed to become a failure. You've made nothin good of yourself, of your craven existence. I'll tell you what you really are: the weak filth who only does what he is told, a thrall to his primitive desires and the unquestioned words of others. You are the coward who would hold down innocent children in the sands of Arkoma and laugh in their final screamin moments."

The man's head suddenly whipped around to face Nelsa and his eyes shot open in horror. He opened his mouth to curse, but stopped dead. Only Ciro's panicked eyes darted around on his frozen expression. His black and gold robes—his stala's projection—collapsed to the ground, leaving all of his pale flesh exposed.

Nelsa looked him up and down and then clicked her tongue. "Ah, you caosin cretin. You're mine now."

CHAPTER TWENTY-FOUR

Ensnared

Nelsa pushed herself up from the chair and stood above Ciro. Controlling his body through his corpus, she moved his head and kept his eyes open so that they followed her.

"Who am I?" she taunted, answering his trapped thoughts. "Don't you recognise me? Oh, of course not. But you wouldn't even recognise my spliced form beneath this disguise. Perhaps you recognise their faces."

Nelsa commanded a projection window to appear before the incapacitated man. It blocked his view of her for a moment, but she needed him to watch as he held down her daughter and revelled in her death. In the death of her son, then her love. She cast the projection away, but fed the scene into his mind on a constant loop.

"You're completely helpless," Nelsa continued, cold and grievous. "Just like my love Teequin. Just like my children, Colquin and Kayli. Say their names. Do it." She relinquished control of his mouth so that he could talk freely.

"You caosin whore! You'll rue the—gahh."

Nelsa played with his nerves so he suffered the ut-most amount of torment possible whilst doing no phys-ical harm. She kept him conscious and his mouth free to squeal. No one could hear them in here. Even if they could, such sounds were not uncommon in Ciro's chambers, or this entire fortress for that matter. Nelsa leant in and growled: "Say their names."

"Te..Teequin," he stuttered. "Colquin. Kay..Kayli."

"That's a good coward." Nelsa twisted his corpus to inflict another wave of unbearable pain. The man sat there unable to move, screaming in agony, his eyes forcefully kept open in horror. "You're never gonna leave this room alive, Ciro. I'm bestowin you the de-cency of that knowledge."

Nelsa stepped back from him to get a better look. "Now, while your fate is certain agony till certain death, I do have to keep you livin for a little while longer, just whilst I take care o' some things. Besides, can't go destroyin your corpus. I suggest you try and find some kinda peace with the little time you have left. If you can even think through the pain."

Nelsa let the torment continue, this time without interruption, but she'd had enough of his screams and shut his mouth. She collapsed back into the chair with a heavy sigh. A part of her thought she'd never make it this far and that she'd be the one imprisoned inside her own flesh. The other part greatly coveted the power over this man, yet now that it had arrived, a bitter taste brewed on her tongue. Her stomach twisted.

"You did well, Nelsa," Maasi said. *"If you can handle it,*

search his corpus for any information on the heirloom."

Nelsa leaned on the intention to find anything about the heirloom just as she would search through her own mind. She found nothing. *"He's just a useless thrall. That knowledge must solely rest with Salazano himself. Perhaps Belva as well."*

"Caosi."

"I can't believe we still don't even know what we're stealin," MoonKidd said. *"You sure we should go through with this?"*

"We'll just have to find out what it is once you're inside the coscraft like we planned. Alright, Nel, time to scan him to update your chameleon. It'll take a little while. Belva and Salazano have arrived up there and the coscraft with the heirloom is on time to descend in three hours. Until then, give yourself a break from dealin with…"

All Nelsa could manage was: *"Understood."* She sat there for a long moment. Eventually, MoonKidd's voice came to her mind.

"Well he got what he wanted in the end didn't he?"

"And what's that?" Nelsa asked. She looked away from the frozen man in perpetual agony and rubbed her forehead.

"Pervert got dominated. Despite an imminent death, he's probably secretly lovin this."

"It ain't no secret," Nelsa said. *"As soon as I took control of his corpus he got the service he paid for."*

Everyone, including her, shared a grim laugh. Nelsa felt guilty for doing so, but it was all she could do to cope with getting the first sliver of vengeance. She would not be laughing when her revenge struck Belva and Salazano. That'd make her no better than them.

If only she got the chance…

CHAPTER TWENTY-FIVE

Falling Apart

"A pity you never join us for the revelries," a voice said. "What became of that whore? Any chance of me renting her or is she too *cold* for that?"

"Her corpse is lying in my chambers," Ciro said. "Didn't have time to cast her into the void. If you're really into such depravity then by all means, I'll let you inside."

Wreathed in the disguise and stolen stala of Ciro Salazano, Nelsa stood amongst the other gold guards. Most were human, only some were tall illuavans, but all were adorned in their black and gold plated armour. They were positioned in long columns on an extended platform that jutted from a high tower of the moon fortress. Disguised as the Padrino's nephew, Nelsa waited at the forefront of the gathering for the heirloom's arrival. The same woman who had approached her at the bar spoke again.

"A true pity," the woman said, smiling fondly. "She possessed quite the alluring aura."

Nelsa scoffed. "Or perhaps your mind was just too

transformed by all the cosgaze you injected. Her looks were nothing but a deceit." She ignored the woman's further comments and stared out over the edge.

Beyond the moon's rim, past the black gulf, hung the planet Arkoma. Half of it was swallowed in eternal blackness, whilst the rest of the world bathed in starlight, gleaming a murky brown orange where the darker broiling clouds did not touch. In the distance, on the planet's misty orange edge, shone the grey sphere of Arkoma's only other moon, Akra. Two Families had their own castles upon its lifeless surface, whilst Sanguul was for Salazano and Lecara—whose fortress was on the other side.

She looked back up at the many shiny vessels flying around the castle like a swarm of mindless sentinels protecting their hive and lord. Growing agitated, Nelsa checked the coscraft's schedule through her connection to Ciro's corpus. It should be descending from its long journey across the galaxy any moment now. From here, she wouldn't be able to see the vessel materialising back into existence upon a pale green river, though she could imagine its beauty. A slight tingling spread across her body just thinking of ascending to that higher dimension. She'd only travelled that way once in her life before, but that was enough to leave a permanent mark on her vital.

Nelsa glanced back over the platform packed with guards and up to the peak of the fortress. *"They still haven't come yet,"* she said. *"What's goin on, Maasi? Do you hear or see anythin?"*

"Nothin yet."

As though to calm her fears, there was sudden movement at the far end of the platform. The massive golden gate melted away and Salazano strode out. Belva followed close behind and to his left, and his personal gold guard marched further back.

Her eyes narrowed as she focused on Salazano and saw the violet shimmer. *"Caosi! It's just a projection of himself! Salazano isn't actually comin!"*

"What do you mean he's not comin?" Maasi replied.

Nelsa's eyes shot up to the tallest pillar of the fortress. *"Salazano. He's still up there!"*

"Why would he do that?" Maasi asked. *"Unless he means to send the projection of himself down to the planet to accompany the heirloom. If that's the case it doesn't matter. We can still move ahead with the plan and steal it once they arrive down here."*

"But I need—" Nelsa cut herself off. Her panic was so heightened she almost let it slip.

"You need what?"

"Nothin." She focused her sight past Salazano. *"Belva is actually here. Salazano must have sent him to escort the heirloom. But why?"*

"It doesn't matter now," Maasi said. *"Just focus on maintainin yourself. We can only wait to see what happens and react accordingly."*

As the gleam of Salazano passed each row of guards, they snapped around to face their lord. Every two seconds came a sound of feet stamping into place. Even Nelsa obliged when it was her turn and she faced the man who had ordered the execution of her family.

Regal robes that constantly rolled like waves of liquid gold draped over Salazano's tall form. His fingernails were fashioned void black like his smooth long hair, and though his cruel eyes appeared the same, they were just a dark shade of brown against his pale face.

He stopped ahead of Nelsa and scoffed. *"Your attempts to appear lordly are ever a disappointment, Ciro."* Salazano's thoughts cast to the mind of Ciro which instantly forwarded them to Nelsa. *"How you have the same blood flowing through your veins will forever be a mystery."*

Armed with the knowledge from Ciro's corpus and brain, Nelsa answered, *"Just what have I done now to add to your further ill judgement of me, Uncle?"*

"Your existence," he coldly answered. The Padrino only kept Ciro around for torment. *"Did you think I wouldn't notice the mess you left behind on Arkoma? I'm done cleaning up after you and your embarrassments to this family. Your depravity is at an end. If you do anything to tarnish my reputation again you shall join all your dead whores in the cold choking void!"* Even though he had not spoken aloud, Salazano made sure to turn around and flash a scowl of his dark eyes.

Nelsa said nothing, giving only a slight nod in acknowledgement. Her gaze slipped past him and landed upon the beast. Belva held his deformed hand against his golden vest. The gloved hand pulled a glowing cig from his grinning mouth. Knowing that he was staring at her through his corpus, she stared straight back into those eyeless dark hollows.

The temptation tortured her.

Belva was really here. Right in front of her, unlike Salazano. She could do it right now. She could get justice for her love, her children. Her family. She could end the waking nightmares. The perpetual unrest of knowing that he still lived while they were dead. All she had to do was form a pistola and put Marston's bullet right in the fiend's skull.

No. Jasolle's words echoed in her mind: *"Revenge is best delivered cold, like the void."* Nelsa stopped herself from forming the pistola. Belva wasn't enough. Salazano wasn't here. Her vengeance required them both. Nelsa let Belva live, for now. She hoped she wouldn't regret it.

Her stala suddenly marked the coscraft carrying the heirloom beginning its descent. The vessel fell from the great above like some winged celestial creature slicing through the night before it silently halted at the end of the platform. A section of the curved silver hull dissolved into a violet mist, falling and solidifying into steps. The entrance into the coscraft gaped open.

After a moment of stillness, Nelsa risked speaking up. She tried her best to make Ciro seem disinterested. "Are we to stand here until Arkoma's Star collapses and burns us all? What are we doing?"

Salazano said nothing, peering ahead at the suspended vessel. Then, like a star flowing down a waterfall at night, a woman adorned in glittering white and golden robes glided down the stairs and across the platform until she stopped before Salazano. She bowed gracefully, then stood proudly tall, eyes gleaming like sapphire gems.

"Who the caosi is this?" Nelsa sent the thought to Maasi to find out.

"I don't know," the coavlen replied. *"That face isn't in their nexus. Must be some noble Velutran who carries the heirloom. That jewel around her neck would certainly be well-placed amongst Sals other hoards. It even resembles the one that hangs off his own neck."*

Nothing else came out of the coscraft save two guards. Their robes glittered like the woman's and they bore golden scimitars crossed upon their backs.

Nelsa looked back through the information in her mind provided by their warlif employer: the heirloom will be the only thing of importance on that coscraft. Then it struck her.

"Maasi," Nelsa said. *"She's the heirloom."*

CHAPTER TWENTY-SIX

Astarina Salazano

"*Steal her?*" Maasi cried. "*A human?*"

Salazano gave the woman a soft bow of his head in return. "Welcome to this humble abode in the wild Frontier, Astarina. I hope your journey was pleasant and that Costhrall tended your vital."

"Thank you, Father," Astarina said, lifting her head and regaining her regal posture.

"*Father?!*" Nelsa shouted in thought.

"*Salazano has fathered plenty of children before,*" Jasolle interjected. "*He keeps the bastards scattered across his domain like pets. But she is not from the Frontier. He's brought her all the way from the Velutra. Perhaps he believes her to be a purer, finer heir and is precious as a result.*"

"*A bastard,*" Maasi repeated. "*His years are wanin, and so he must mean for her to take over. Perhaps he does so openly now as an affront to the other Families. The Salazano line will continue in its dominance.*"

"Let us not tarry here," Salazano said. "Come, follow me to my tower so I can look upon you with my own eyes. I can already see that glint of myself in yours. But

I would have you see this keep before we venture down to Arkoma. It will, after all, pass to you once I am gone."

"May Costhrall delay that for many years to come, Father." Astarina smiled like an elegant star gleaming upon the surface of a kind eye. Then she turned to Nelsa and her smile faded, if only a little. "And this must be my dearly long lost cousin. I am sorry about your father, Ciro. A tragedy for everyone who proudly wears our name."

The aftermath of her words sat in a prolonged silence until Nelsa suddenly realised words were expected of her. "It was many years ago," she said, startled. "You have nothing to apologise for. In truth it is I who should be sorry for how my father tarnished our Family's reputation."

Once she'd gained control of Ciro's corpus, Nelsa saw that Salazano had his own brother—Ciro's father—murdered for supposed heresy against the Family. Ciro suspected that there was never any betrayal. It was just Sal consolidating power and putting an end to the brotherly rivalry that had plagued them since they were youths. The only reason Ciro was kept in the family was to make him an example for anyone else who considered dissent. That was just how Salazano did things.

"We need not inherit the burdens of our fathers," Astarina said. "A new dawn is always rising somewhere in the cosmos."

"Already wise beyond your years." Salazano placed a proud hand on her shoulder. "Alas, I am an old man and have many burdens. But I take no offence, dear daughter. Unfortunately, Ciro here has inherited quite a few sins of his father. Perhaps your compassion and fierceness will be able to cleanse them."

"Yes, Father."

Salazano guided Astarina and they started back down the platform between the lines of guards. Sal made sure to give Ciro a foul leer as he sent words to his mind. *"Fall in behind us, dear nephew. If you behave then perhaps you'll live to see the day she becomes your lord. I'll be sure to sharpen her edge when it comes to dealing with you."*

Nelsa stood there in a daze. *"They aren't goin now!"* she cried. *"What am I gonna do?"*

"Do as you're told and follow em!" Maasi said. *"You heard him, he only wants to show off the keep. Then they'll both come down here together. Bide your time!"*

"Are your legs suddenly broken?" a voice said. Nelsa blinked and focused on Belva and his eyeless scowl. "You best fall in, or I'll break them for you and drag you after your uncle while every other gold guard laughs."

Nelsa glowered, as did her Ciro disguise. "That's funny," she said. "They're always laughing at you when you're not looking—oh, you didn't see that did you? Eyeless caosi."

Nelsa walked off, but kept watch behind her as Belva's dead expression watched her go.

"What are you doin?" Maasi said. *"Don't do nothin to give yourself away."*

Nelsa tensed for retaliation, but Belva's hard countenance broke into a grin. The man who put the blade into the backs of her children and her love walked behind her as he playfully hummed.

CHAPTER TWENTY-SEVEN

Walk With the Enemy

"Are you joyous at the arrival of your long-lost relative? You don't look it."

Nelsa kept her eyes ahead but could see Belva through her stala. He'd caught up to her and now matched her pace. "Are you terribly sad that your lord has a new favourite? You look it."

"Quite the contrary," Belva chuckled. "I was beginning to think his obsession with me unhealthy. Alas, when the bitter day finally comes and I must bid farewell to my Padrino, his heir shall be a fine replacement. Do not fret, I'll continue to whisper of your true worthless nature. You never know, I have a feeling in my vital that you may not see the day. You may be cast into the void like all your whores."

"Plagues don't have vitals," Nelsa growled.

Belva laughed again, then fell grimly silent. The cavities of his missing eyes were harshly fixed on her. "Is it last night's carousing that emits this bitter aura from you, or is it just the presence of our visitor, the exquisite Astarina? You do not seem yourself, Ciro."

Nelsa's stomach dropped at the accusation. Her mind flashed back to Ciro's chambers where he remained conscious and frozen in his chair, perpetually in torment, yet safe from discovery. Doubt maliciously crept in.

"I'm just caosin tired of your antics, Belva," Nelsa said, trying to recover from his suspicions. "You have worn my vital down to a thin rotting strand. I long for the day our Padrino grants you permission to sever it completely and rid me of this troubling existence."

Belva's laugh returned with a vengeance. "Such a wounded little thing you are. Ah, you will never know how much delight it truly gives me."

"If only you didn't carve out your own eyes you could see me smiling."

"Ah yes," he said. "That old fable. I cut my own eyes out to terrify my enemies. They say I ate them too." He snickered. "No, I did not do this to myself. I was once forced to travel through the Void Realm. I saw too much. As punishment for all the insight I gained, Malnetha stole my eyes. It always claims something for those who dare enter its domain."

Nelsa stopped and looked across into those dark hollow sockets. More than the eyes had been removed—all the skin around them had been carved wider to appear more disfigured. It didn't matter whether what he was saying was true or not.

"So that explains your madness. Malnetha gifted you with the Mind Rot. Don't mind me if I keep my distance from now on." Nelsa resisted the recurring temptation to put the bullet in his head and kept walking.

She passed through the grand archway into the keep
and caught up to Salazano and Astarina. The Padrino
frequently stopped to point out important sections of
the fortress. With every passing moment Nelsa's fear
of getting exposed grew and every step felt as though
another crushing weight pressed against her chest.

The party eventually entered a grav-sheath that carried them to the very pinnacle of the keep. Nelsa exited
first with Belva and several other guards and they began
to move down a grand hallway of golden carved pillars.
The Padrino called out.

"You are excused, Ciro. You may return to whatever
depraved fornicating we interrupted."

Stunned, Nelsa turned back to Salazano. Her stala
projected behind her to the black and gold gates, beyond
which dwelt Salazano's true body. Precisely where she
had to get to.

Nelsa re-focused on Astarina and asked, "When will
we depart for Arkoma?"

"You're no longer needed for that, nephew," Sal said.
"Or should I say, you never were. I just wanted you to
behold the radiant Astarina."

"An honour to meet your vital, Ciro," she said with a
soft curtsy. Guided by her father, the pair went to move
past Nelsa down the hallway.

"What the caosi am I goin to do?" Nelsa cried to the
others. *"I've gotta do somethin now!"*

"You can't do anythin up there on your lonesome," Maasi
replied.

"Then get yourselves up here!"

"No! We're abortin this," Maasi ordered. *"Take the out they're given you and head back to Ciro's chambers. Then leave the fortress on the next grav-train back down here."*

At that moment, the defence systems of Ciro's quarters alerted her as they were abruptly overpowered. A gold guard entered and beheld Ciro incapacitated in a chair. The guard rushed forward to aid him, and Nelsa panicked. She pierced his brain and heart, ending Ciro's life.

"I can't do that, Maasi," Nelsa shuddered. *"The ruse is up. I can't go back."*

CHAPTER TWENTY-EIGHT

Hostage

Nelsa caught the sudden look of horror on Belva's horrid face. Before he or anyone else could do anything, she screamed her threats for everyone to hear.

"This is a life eater warhead!" Her disguise collapsed to her true form and her robes peeled back to reveal the red orb strapped to her chest. "One wrong move and this ruptures, devourin all of ye and this entire caosin fortress! I die and so do all of ye!"

"What are you doin?" Maasi cried.

"What I gotta, Maasi. I'm sorry everyone. Sorry I didn't tell you all bout this. I'm sorry I lied. Don't even think about comin up here."

"How the void did she get a life eater?" Maasi shouted to the others. *"Did you give it to her, Marston?"*

"No," he replied. *"She must have got it when I—"*

Nelsa severed her corpus' communication.

"I thought I could smell something different about you," Belva said, grinning.

"What are your demands?" Salazano growled.

"You," she spat. "Get out here now. I'm sick of lookin

at your projection."

"I can't do that."

"Then I'll rupture this and devour her!"

"I'm not coming out there. You would only kill us all, Astarina included."

"I don't need to be the one doin the killin," Nelsa answered. "Kill yourself in front o' me and I'll let her go. She can fulfil her purpose and become the new Padrino."

Belva snickered. "You don't have the vital. The courage."

"Try me."

He sneered. "And where did you procure such a thing? Been dealing with the zenlians have we?"

Nelsa tapped the orb strapped to her chest and it started to leak a black mist laden with white ash. "Keep talkin, wretch. Tell your master you can smell the leakin nivlon."

Belva gave an impressive scoff. "It seems she's quite serious, Padrino. What is its range? Twenty metres? Ten? That little life eater may swallow all of us here into the blackness of the Void Realm, yet I'd argue the grav-sheaths beyond those doors would be able to hold it off in time and keep our Padrino safe. If it even reaches that far. Even from right outside his very doors, it wouldn't reach his throne. A shame. You were so close. You're a fool for coming here, for thinking you could get away with this. You're going to die now." Belva formed a short blade from his stala. "I'm going to enjoy flaying your flesh."

"Stop!" Salazano ordered. "You want me. If you kill

you have no leverage. You won't let yourself die without taking me first. I won't attack you, lest you trigger the warhead out of desperation. It seems we're at an impasse."

"Do all ye hear this?" Nelsa yelled to the surrounding gold guards. "He has no care for your life. You will all die if he does not come out. What say ye now? Will ye continue to serve your Padrino?"

Grim looks passed between the guards, but they all remained silent where they stood.

Salazano scoffed. "Do you not know of the oaths my gold guards swear? Their bodies are bound to my mind and my vital until death. They live only to serve me. And Belva, well. He has no fear of death, do you friend?"

Belva shook his eyeless face in agreement.

"And what of your daughter?" Nelsa narrowed her focus, grasping for control. "You do not want her harmed but you're unwillin to sacrifice your life for hers!"

"She knows the ways of our Family," he said, coldly. "I have a great many things to accomplish to secure the safekeeping of my Family before I depart this corporeal flesh. Things only I can do. So, what is to be done? If you mean to rupture the life eater, do it now and spare us the suspense."

Nelsa was lost, her thoughts muddled in chaotic confusion. She had to get to Salazano, but could not. He was the true target—not this heirloom, this woman, Astarina. She'd resolved to die, but now she could not do so knowing Salazano would survive. Her focus shifted to

Belva again and his silent grin.

"Kill your pet then," she said in a neurotic state. "I want to watch you kill Belva as I watched him kill my family."

A confused expression grew on Belva's face. "Your family? Which one? I'm responsible for the demise of so many."

"Silnur," Nelsa snarled her family name with quivering rage.

Belva burst out laughing, then fell silent as he eyed his master with a cruel grin.

"Well," Salazano said, his cold countenance showing more expression than ever before. "Isn't this interesting? Layli Silnur, I never thought I'd actually see you again. You spliced yourself into this...cheap form. Addict and Duelist Nelsa Nolstar, if I'm not mistaken. You were so beautiful before. A shame. You've had a place in my mind ever since you stole from me. Since I had to teach you a lesson."

"Now I'm here to teach you one. Kill Belva or I kill your daughter."

Salazano's projection leered across at Astarina then back to Nelsa. "And you would relinquish her if I obliged?"

"I would," Nelsa said, unsure if it was a lie. "Once I'm in the clear. But if you don't, and quickly, then I'll rupture this thing and drag her into Malnetha's locker."

Salazano eyed her intensely, then he turned to his daughter. "Forgive me, Astarina, yet I cannot yield to this knave. We would all die. You must understand this."

Astarina's aghast mouth closed and she held her head high. "It is as you taught me, Father. We do not concede to traitors."

"I am sorry, my dear daughter."

"Get out here now!" Nelsa cried. "Or I'm gonna do it!"

"You do realise, Layli, that this is all your fault," Belva said. "If you had never stolen from Salazano to begin with then your family would still be alive. This vengeance won't do your vital any good. You're not rotten like me. It'll only leave you feeling more hollow."

"Shut up, filth!" Nelsa screamed. The floor turned to sand and everyone else disappeared except for Belva. She stood where they died. A soft wind scratched off the top layer of sand and blew dust against the orange landscape and clear blue sky. Gritting her teeth, she pointed a trembling finger at Belva as though she held her pistola.

"Oh, you're deadly," he cackled, then he took a step forward. "But you're too weak to rupture that life eater. No, you're going to be alive for a long time. I'll make certain of that. I'll add your screams to the melody I created with your children. It soothes me to sleep each night."

"Where do you think you're goin to go when you die?" Nelsa muttered in a slow rage. "The Void Realm? Or the Cos Realm?"

Belva tilted his head and pointed to his eyeless hollows. "To the black locker, of course. I'll be certain to say hello to your family when I get there. If Malnetha has left any shred of them behind for me to play with."

Nelsa steadied her jittery hand. "If you want to die smilin like a slave of Malnetha, then by all means."

Belva chuckled, head twitching as he stalked forward, stretching his limbs. "What better way could one—"

In an instant, Nelsa formed a pistola around her finger and fired. Violet light flashed, followed by a crunching, warped screech as the bullet pierced straight into Belva's forehead and exploded out the back. Half his skull flew off with it. The eyeless head fell to the floor with a wet thud.

Belva, the Hand of Chaos, returned to the eternal black.

CHAPTER TWENTY-NINE

One Remains

Nelsa's pistola remained fixated on Belva's corpse but all she could see was her love and her children bleeding and dead in the sand.

Her mind snapped and the desert vanished.

The closest gold guard, who happened to be the woman from before, formed a blade. Nelsa whipped her pistola around and pointed it at Astarina.

"Stop!" Salazano bellowed.

"How do you want her to die?" Nelsa roared. "With half her head blown off or devoured by the void?" She tapped the orb on her chest with her free hand. "Go ahead and caosin try me! I'll kill all of ye!"

Salazano smirked. He looked pitifully down at his servant, no longer able to serve, then back up to Nelsa. His hard countenance solidified. "And what is your plan now? I'm still not coming out."

Nelsa panted hard, trying to control her disordered thoughts. Then a river of clarity washed through her mind. She had achieved one sliver of her vengeance, yet there was still one more she had to claim. Salazano would not trade his life for his daughter's and Nelsa could not trade hers. The special bullet and life eater strapped to her chest had got her this far but no further. Adrenaline rushed through her with the realisation that she had to get out of here alive.

"How about a duel?" Nelsa said. She didn't know how the thought came into her mind. It was all she could think of to get another chance at killing him. "Ten steps to doom. Do you have any honour left to honour the rites of the Sacred Duel?"

"I'd heard of your growing duelling exploits throughout the city," Salazano said. Then he laughed in agreement. "Why don't we do it now? I can save you from the prolonged dread."

"No," Nelsa glared. "Tomorrow. Where they died. Till then, the woman is mine." Nelsa gestured for Astarina to step closer. The woman complied, gliding to her like a Sage.

"You try to flee Arkoma and I'll know," Salazano said. "There's nowhere in the Frontier where you'll be able to hide from me. Splicing your face won't save you again. I'll find you and reclaim her."

"You try to cheat or back your way out of our duel and you'll find her dead. Or maybe she'll just disappear into the black."

Salazano scowled. "You will fail then as you failed here. It is foolish to think you can get away with your life."

"Failed?" Nelsa barked a laugh. "I got that dead fiend there, as well as your dear nephew. This has actually turned out for the better. I get to let you live in fear. The shadow of Malnetha will linger above your old head. You best tell your guards to move now."

"Let her pass," Salazano muttered and the surrounding guards stepped aside. "This is not a concession, Astarina. I will kill this wretch myself. I will keep you alive, you have my promise on that."

"I trust in you, Father," Astarina said. At the prompt of Nelsa's pistola she turned and walked ahead towards the grav-sheath they had arrived in.

"Trust in me and my life eater," Nelsa said. "You want to take over Arkoma one day? You'll do as I say."

With that they entered the grav-sheath and Nelsa commanded it with her corpus. Before it cast them away she faced Salazano. He stood in the ornate black and golden hallway like a forlorn statue. Tomorrow he would lay broken and bleeding in the thirsty sands.

For now she had to escape.

CHAPTER THIRTY

Escape

Nelsa landed at the bottom of the grav-sheath some-where in the centre of the keep.

"Take out your corpus now!" she yelled, pointing the pistola at Astarina. After a silent scowl, she obliged and a violet mist swirled around her neck. Then she winced as it pierced the skin and pulled out a star shaped device the size of her fingernail. Disconnected, Astarina's stala robes collapsed to the floor like raining violet sand. She handed the corpus to Nelsa who tossed it away, destroying it with a shot from her pistola.

"Your tarmin next," Nelsa commanded, gesturing to the silver band around Astarina's wrist. "That's what you fancy Velutrans call em, ain't it?" Nelsa had both of hers hanging off her hips in radiant orbs.

"I was never a Velutran," she muttered. Astarina touched the silver band with her other hand and it rippled like a wave losing its rigid shape. In a moment it fell to the ground. "Father raised me in the ways of the Frontier. Will you not do me the decency of covering me?"

A mist drifted off Nelsa's stala and it covered Astarina in plain black robes. "I don't care about your decency, but I gotta keep you in line somehow."

Nelsa's stala pushed Astarina forward in a sprint, and she followed behind. Nelsa accessed the schematics of the castle and headed towards the closest coscraft landing platform.

"I need a coscraft up here now!" Nelsa cried, reactivating her corpus connection to the others. *"I need to get outta here. I've sent you my live location."*

"What happened?" Maasi replied.

"I've taken Astarina hostage."

"Hostage? With what?"

"A life eater. I also used your bullet, Mars. I'm in real trouble if I don't get outta here quick. Are you comin or not?"

"We'll get you outta there," Maasi said. *"Everythin will be aight. We'll pick you up as soon as we can get there. Give us three minutes."*

"Just hurry!"

As they fled, the dusty red terrain of the moon flashed by in glimpses beyond the castle's impenetrable black and gold walls. Circular craters of varying sizes marred the hills, plains and valleys. Over it all lay a stark disquiet. Fortified towers sprung out of immense battlements, violet beams of light casting into the black sky from their peaks. They harvested nivlon to maintain the fabricated atmosphere and gravity. Out from the castle's front gate, outlaws hung in the void for their crimes.

She wouldn't be that lucky.

Nelsa and Astarina shot through other grav-sheaths,

passing lawkeeps and civilians who looked on with horror. No one dared approach as the Padrino had ordered.

"Sal must really love you," Nelsa said as they ran. "No doubt he has many heirs he could choose from, but he treasures you for some reason."

"Who knows," Astarina heaved. "Perhaps I was just the first to ripen."

They stopped at an intersection and Nelsa looked over the edge at the inside of the keep. Bridges and pathways spanned everywhere, and against the black buttresses patches of lush flora blossomed their verdant green. At the very bottom, like a field of black stone cut into many uneven shapes, sat the lesser dwellings of the castle's inhabitants.

"Some plan you had," Astarina mocked. "I can see your brain scrambling through your eyes."

"I'll see your brain splattered if you don't shut your mouth."

"Then you'll never get to my father. Surely you have a plan other than facing him in a duel?"

"Don't fret, I'll put your daddy in the dirt tomorrow." Nelsa set off again down another bridge.

They passed through a set of gates onto a large platform full of waiting coscrafts. Some people scurried into their crafts, while those who boldly remained glared at them. Nelsa stopped their sprinting and glanced around for any sign of her friends.

"Maasi," she hailed for the fifth time. *"Where are you?"*
No answer.

"What the caosi is goin on? Maasi? Why aren't you

answerin me? Mars? Is anyone there?"

Nelsa's panic took over. Her lungs burned like the inside of a star, and her stomach ached as though she were pregnant with pestilence. Her eyes darted wildly.

"It's not too late to stop this," Astarina said. "I can grant you clemency from my father's wrath."

"Shut your mouth!" Nelsa snapped and a piece of her stala peeled off and sealed Astarina's mouth. "I'm thinkin."

Her heightened paranoia glimpsed movement from a nearby war-torn coscraft. It looked like the head of some monstrous creature, with two long barrels for eyes pointed straight at her. From the inside of its open jaw, a group of equally ragged humans approached her.

"Oi!" Nelsa cried as they kept moving towards her. One look at them told her their profession. "Oi! Stay back, ye bounty hunting serpents. Ain't ye heard Salazano's commands?"

"We heard him aight," one said through a thin smirk. "Told everyone to stay clear on account of your life eater and stala piercin bullets. You see the thing is..." A projection of her Wanted poster appeared in his hand for her to see. "That's a pretty hefty reward on your head."

"I'll send us all into the black locker if any of ye take another step closer." Nelsa moved Astarina to the side and tapped the crimson orb attached to her chest. The pistola in her other hand kept swapping its aim between those that approached and back to Astarina.

"Yea, you see, we ain't so sure bout that," a second man said.

"We're willin to wager you're outta those sta-la-piercin bolts," another spoke up.

"Those bullets are a rare thing out in these parts," the fourth and final bounty collector said. "In any part of this galaxy, really. You could probably only afford the one shot for the man you wanted to kill. It seems you've fallen outta Costhrall's fortune there, child."

Nelsa's stomach dropped into the endless abyss and her lie shattered.

They kept stalking closer.

She froze.

"Life eaters also happen to be a rare thing out in the Frontier," the first bounty collector said. "Unless one happens to be acquainted with the zenlians. Terrible things life eaters are. All-consumin. Yet there's quite a bit most don't know about em, especially these civilised folk of Arkoma. For example…"

Nelsa reactively spawned her lumenshield, but at that moment the translucent purple sphere surrounding her and Astarina shattered with a piercing bang. Another blast from one of the coscraft's eyes passed straight through her stala and smote the red sphere attached to her chest. The impact smacked to the ground with a breathless gasp.

Her mind went blank with shock and pain. She wheezed from the blow, ribs that were surely broken aching with each breath. The next thing she knew there were figures all around lashing her with whips. Each one cracked against her stala. Pangs of pain came down on her like a rain of electric fists. Each blow got stronger.

Her defence weakened. Rage grew. Fury.

Nelsa bellowed a guttural scream. "Get the caosi off me!"

She madly thrashed and tried to get to her feet but their whips broke through her frail stala. Wrapping around her wrists, they slammed her back down. Controlling Astarina through her corpus, she attacked one of the Collectors. Astarina was overpowered in a second and whisked out of sight, freed from her control.

Nelsa formed a blade with her mind and hurled it at the closest Collector. It shattered against his armour. Their whips ripped the radiant orbs off her hips and others grabbed her legs and pinned her to the ground. They held her so tight she couldn't even thrash. But they let her scream.

The dregs of her stala protecting her neck were forced aside and something bit her flesh. Like a sapient parasite embedded in her body, it crept through towards her corpus.

"No!" Nelsa cried. "No, no, no, no! Stop! Please!"

The extinguishing of her corpus felt as though all the lights in the universe suddenly went dark. Connections to the nexus and all its information. Severed. Pathways to reach out to her friends. Disconnected. Every memory of her family that she had saved on her corpus. Destroyed. Now she only had the memories and emotions that were naturally stored in her brain. After years of veroni abuse, little was left.

All the tiny cryluns that had once protected her as a complete stala now fell to the floor as raining shards of violet glass. The defeat left her naked and exposed to the world.

The shadow of the first collector fell over Nelsa and he looked down at her with a confused expression. "What was I sayin?" he said. "Ah yes. For example, a blast right to the core of the life eater with just the right amount of nivlon will render it defunct. I had to coat the blast with a stala-piercin bolt, but I think it did the trick quite marvellously. A sizable bounty on your head. No doubt it was worth the expenditure. Salazano pays well." He laughed and all the others joined in.

Nelsa snarled up at the man like a rabid creature. Then she broke and groaned in despair as she wept. She had no idea what had happened to her friends, but she had a feeling she was about to join them in death.

CHAPTER THIRTY-ONE

Collected

The whips of the bounty collectors forced Nelsa to her knees and she moaned in agony. A blackness shot out from the collector's stala and formed a set of chains that bound Nela's arms behind her back, wrapped around her neck, and extended in a misty chain back to his hands.

Duelling for ismo was one thing, but she was no warrior. She was unaccustomed to physical pain and defeat. Not even her vital was a fighter, not anymore. She had given up so long ago. Just when she thought she'd found a strand of strength, when she'd stumbled across some hope, it had been trampled and spat upon. She knelt there, mouth hanging open and silent in defeat.

The craving for a drink of veroni started to stir in the pit of her stomach. She needed something to escape all this if they would not grant her a quick death.

One of the bounty collectors approached Astarina, crouching and covering herself a short distance away. He relinquished a small part of his stala to cover her in plain white robes.

"My sincerest thanks," Astarina said, doing her best to

regain her regal composure.

"So you're his precious, aye," one of the collectors said. "What a treat."

"Cut it out, Yop," the collector leader said. Then he gave Astarina a soft bow of the head. "It is our pleasure, ma'am."

"You took quite the risk," she said, tone changing to one of disapproved royalty. "Not only with your own life but mine and those around. Explain yourselves."

"Risks are our trade," he said. "When large sums of ismo are involved, it's most always worth the gamble."

"My life is worth more than that. But I shall overlook that now, considering the outcome. You have dealt with cursed tech like that life eater before?"

The lead bounty collector spat some baccy on the floor and scoffed. "This ain't our first time collectin wanted vitals, my regal sweetness. I once seen a life eater large enough to devour this entire castle whole. I stood on the edge of that terrible sphere o' darkness as it turned everythin into nothin. A bad fate that is. One I ain't ever wanna receive."

Astarina met Nelsa's gaze and a thin grin slithered upon her face. "Pitiful thing. You were so close. Alas, not today."

"Shut your Velutran whore mouth," Nelsa muttered. "I should have put a bullet in your head when I got the chance."

"Alas, not today," Astarina repeated, and her smile grew venomous. "Not tomorrow, nor any day after. Father will lock you away somewhere in the void and watch you rot until the end of your miserable days."

"If that means I don't have to listen to you anymore then so be it."

Astarina scoffed.

"I suppose we should take this lass to your lord so he can have a word with her," the lead collector said.

A coscraft came to a rapid stop overhead and shot down a dozen gold guards in grav-sheaths. The leader of that unit glided over. "We'll take it from here, scavengers."

"You couldn't handle her before," he said, placing a hand on Nelsa's head. "What makes you think you can now?" He spat baccy on the floor. "We've taken care of her corpus and all, but we best escort her the whole way. Can never be too careful in our profession. We don't want her pullin any little tricks on you, do we now, my regal sweetness?"

The gold guard stepped closer and yelled, "Speak to her again and you'll have that foul tongue cut out!"

"Silence!" Astarina commanded. "My father will very much desire to thank them. Their identities were surely confirmed when they entered the keep?"

"They were," the guard answered, bowed face marked with fear.

A projection grew out from the armour of the silenced gold guard like a misty wraith. "I will very much wish to thank them with my true presence," he said. "And the *scavenger* is correct. We cannot afford another ruinous error on behalf of my pathetic guards. Bounty collectors are the backbone of the Frontier. Now lead our esteemed guests to me. I am glad you are safe, Astarina. I own my decision to not come out, but I don't think my vital could have suffered your loss."

"I am sorry to have burdened you, Father," she said. "We are now indebted to my saviours here, though it is not a bitter debt but one gladly paid."

"Indeed, they shall be suitably rewarded." Salazano looked down and met Nelsa's eyes. "We'll have to delay our duel, what a pity. Wretched little thing. You need not fear death. I plan on honouring the late Belva's wishes and keeping you alive for some time, unlike the mercifully swift death I gave your family. Alas, I must begin a search for a new tormenting hand. You have robbed me of mine. Perhaps I shall have a turn myself and see what I have learned over the years of watching Belva."

The projection of Salazano disappeared.

"Cover her," Astarina ordered, gesturing to the naked Nelsa.

"The one that threatened your life here?" the bounty collector said, confused.

"Yes. It is improper for her to walk through this keep displayed as such. I'll give her the decency, though she doesn't deserve it. Cover her and follow. Hurry."

Astarina turned and began walking away.

The bounty collector did as he was asked and he wreathed Nelsa in plain black attire. He then tugged at the chain in his hands, sending a cold shock through her body that abruptly stood her upright against her own volition.

"Payback for your antics is just beginnin, darlin," he said laughing. "Some plan you had comin in here all by your lonesome. A fool without friends, if you ask me. You ain't got the Mind Rot do you? Malnetha got you in its black grasp, that's for sure."

He tugged at the chain again, forcing Nelsa to take a step forward. She got the hint and kept walking, but every couple of steps he tugged at it anyway just for a chuckle.

All she wanted was a drink. To numb the pain. The failure.

CHAPTER THIRTY-TWO

Finding New Employment

Nelsa stood before the golden doors of Salazano's sanctum. When the gate cracked and started to fold inwards, Astarina pressed forward and the bounty collector forced Nelsa in after her. The binds that held her arms shocked her every few seconds and the collar choking her neck made it hard to breathe.

Directly ahead rose a tall black and golden throne. Golden wings curving down from either side held the throne suspended in the air. Salazano sat there in his golden robes and long hair falling about him like a curtain of night, blending into the shades of his lustrous decorations. Three high arched windows behind the throne depicted the heraldry of the Sal family in gleaming shards of black and gold glass. The floor was polished stone as though some god had spilt the blood of golden stars across a black abyss. An imperceptible window curved around the rest of the room, looking out upon the red plains and horizon of eternal starry night. Though delicate in appearance, the walls were heavily fortified. Beyond them several sentinel coscrafts circled the keep.

Against the backdrop, three figures adorned in black robes swayed, faces hidden by golden masks of glittering jewels. They moved to the melodies emanating from floating orbs that cast sounds throughout the entire chamber. The haunting, rhythmic melody only added to the foreboding doom that crept into Nelsa's vital with every step.

The head bounty collector forced Nelsa to kneel before the throne. The dread increased, but she kept her head held high. Her eyes bent with malice upon Salazano. It was all she had left. Astarina walked forward to the throne and bowed to her father, who smiled and nodded in reply.

"It is great to behold your beauty with my own eyes," he said, with a wry smile. Then he nodded and Astarina stepped to the side and turned to face the chamber.

"I believe payment is due," Salazano said. "As a token of my gratitude for your efforts today, her bounty has been doubled."

"Thank you, my lord," the leader said. "Your generosity is greatly appreciated. A fortuitous fortress this is indeed. We are honoured to be in your presence."

Salazano gave a slightly amused grin. "You need not act unlike your true Frontier selves. That crude tongue is not as affronting to me as you may assume."

"Aye, that's good to hear," the collector said. "We ain't the biggest talkers. Our proficiency is in killin no-goods for ismo." He tugged at the chain and gave Nelsa a sharp gasping shock.

"Indeed." Salazano eyed him hard and then crossed his legs beneath his long flowing robes. "Despite the risk you took with my daughter's life at the hands of this lowly knave, I see it was not truly a risk. You are experienced collectors. It seems I would be foolish not to place you under my employment. Something for your band to consider amongst yourselves."

"There ain't need no for consideration," he said. "I speak for the rest of em when I say you got yourself a deal!"

"Splendid. The information you provided to the fortress security indicates that you came from Bazabarnia hunting the elusive murderer they call Yenne."

"Yea, we all joined up out Bazabarni way years ago. Was in the area lookin for that old scoundrel when that Wanted poster went live for this little thing here. We've been hard pressed of late to tell you the truth. Collectin ain't no easy undertakin that's for caosin sure. We're just glad we got here in time to be of assistance."

"Ah yes," Salazano said, sibilant. "You may relinquish her chains to my command."

"May I be so bold as to ask what you have planned for her?" the Collector said before doin so. "I do tend to fancy meself a pain connoisseur."

"And what would you do if I put you in charge of her punishment? What are some of your favourite techniques?"

"Well," the Collector said, delighted to be indulged. "Assumin you are wantin to keep her alive for a while, I'd probably start with little bursts o' void drownin.

Then maybe I'd do some interior crylun scratchin, you know, just really let her feel as though I'm everywhere inside—that there's nowhere I can't inflict pain. Probably then do some mind stuff, really torment her vital. Oh, and I also have a thing that I like to do where I flay their skin and muscles and replace their veins with crylun rivers. I slowly cut out their organs and fabricate crylun replacements to keep em alive until only the brain is left. Most don't make it that far. Their vitals are too weak and give up by then. Yet somethin tells me this one might last quite a while."

Nelsa's gaze finally dropped from the man on the throne. She stared down at the ground, numb with defeat.

"That is quite the method," Salazano said, rubbing his proud chin. "Very well. I will give you a trial as my torturer. Yet first I would like to attempt my own hand. Now, relinquish those chains to me."

"Yea, about that," the Collector said, voice suddenly hesitant. "The thing is that…uh…well, I don't wanna."

"Excuse me?" Salazano growled.

"You heard me. Are you truly that dull you ain't realise I just been stallin? Why the caosi would I hand over our friend?"

Nelsa's eyes widened and she gasped, but just as she did so everything was devoured by an impenetrable darkness.

CHAPTER THIRTY-THREE

Wasting Words With Revenge

When the darkness swallowed her, Nelsa flinched, recoiling from certain death. But death did not come. A pure nothingness engulfed her. She could not even see her own body and yet she could still feel its weariness and the chains that bound her in place. Her panicked lungs gasped for air, although the atmosphere remained unchanged.

Then the chains broke and her limbs dropped free. A warmth folded in over every part of her hidden body as though she had been guided into the comforting womb of the mother of the cosmos. A solid object wrapped around her forearm and something pierced her flesh, but the darkness still obscured everything.

Sounds came to her as though they seeped in from another universe. Distant and nearby at the same time. Warped screeches, shouts, screams. They had been there all along but the darkness had briefly stolen her senses.

Rivers of light abruptly wove through her mind. A flood of information appeared and drifting between them were strands of connections to other minds. A corpus, reattaching to her brain. She realised that the device on her forearm was an external corpus and stala vault, like she'd given MoonKidd and StarFlower at Belva's dungeon. The warmth around her now was a replenished stala protecting her.

That meant this darkness could only have been one thing.

"Well looky what the great black dragged in," MoonKidd said. *"Go on, everyone wants to hear how dearly you missed me."*

"You all came for me?" Nelsa replied in thought.

"Course we did," Maasi said. *"But we're a little bit busy dealin with these guards for conversin at the moment."*

"How can you move or see in this darkness?" Nelsa asked anyway.

"Told you before that I got it sorted," Marston said. *"Not your external corpus though, I'm afraid. Only got ten seconds left of the Blinder—need to make the most of it!"*

"Feel free to join in!" MoonKidd laughed.

Nelsa stood but the disorientation of the nothingness spun her around. All she could do was listen to the fighting. Amidst the blind mayhem she could hear Salazano bellowing: "Kill them all! Get rid of this darkness!" But after a moment his shouts were silenced.

"Get ready, we ain't done yet!" Marston said. *"And Marston says…let there be light!"*

As though Costhrall itself had descended to reanimate the cosmos back to life, the pure blackness instantly retracted to its detonation point outside the keep. Colour and life returned to the chamber. Nelsa blinked a few times to recover. When she found her footing, she glanced around to assess the situation. The gang had discarded their bounty collecting disguises and fought the last of the gold guards.

StarFlower wielded a mace the size of MoonKidd and bashed the meagre blade of a guard until it cracked. He kept pummeling the guard's armour until it shattered and split his head open. A violet fiery mist wreathed StarFlower's massive form. Nelsa saw through their mind connection that Maasi had reprogrammed Salazano's personal crylun horde in the chamber and divided it amongst them, enhancing their stalas.

She looked over to MoonKidd. The salenai wielded a gatling crygun whose joint rotating barrels were each as large as her muscled forearm and as long as her entire height. They issued a constant barrage of projectiles at the guards who tried to rush her, stopping them dead in their tracks. She fired until she broke their lumenshields and armour and pulverised their bodies into chunks of organic mess.

All the while MoonKidd issued bursts of mad laughter and screams of "Yeehaw!" and "I ain't spank ye hard enough last time?" and the rare "Oh c'mon now, law. That all ye got?"

Maasi was in zais glowing jelly form and two of the coavlen's tentacles pointed at the back of Salazano and Astarina's heads. They knelt upon the polished black and gold floor in nothing but their skin. Salazano bled from his leg, face contorted with agony and a seething bitterness. Marston stood over them, pointing a pistola at each.

Nelsa took a step forward, before stopping in her tracks at the carnage outside the keep. A great mass of coscrafts violently danced with one another all around the castle and in the void above. In just a glance outside, three erupted into violent purple flames before the lifeless void extinguished them. Her stala and the castle's windows protected her eyes from the blinding flashes. A constant rumble thundered through the walls as explosions detonated within the fortress' atmosphere.

"What the void is goin on out there?" Nelsa called to the others. She rushed forward and stood beside Marston. *"Is this your doin as well?"*

"It ain't nothin to do with us," Maasi said. *"It must be one of the other Families makin a move against him. Guess we were bait after all."*

"You sure these doors are sealed, Maasi?" MoonKidd asked.

"It'll hold any guards off for a while. Besides, they got other things to worry about."

StarFlower and MoonKidd finished the last of the gold guards and flew back to the others.

Salazano spat at Nelsa's feet. "Wait, don't tell me. Did Lecara get to you? Did he promise you a way to kill me? Ah, he used my dear Astarina. It seems you've played your part as a mere distraction. Whatever Lecara promised you was a lie. I cannot amend the years of grief I have caused you, but I can give you—"

Nelsa slapped him with the back of her hand. "Twelve years of anguish. Twelve!" She breathed hard through her nose, fighting down her rage. "I'm goin to make you suffer as I have."

Salazano shifted his jaw and smiled. "You have to make examples in positions such as mine. I do not expect you to understand, lowly thieves that you are." He chuckled. "How about instead of stealing something from you, I give you something you are sorely deprived of?"

"You can give me nothin. The only satisfaction I need is your butchered corpse dryin up in the desert!"

"Oh, I'm not so sure about that. Tell me, have you really still not noticed? Have you not earnestly looked into Astarina's eyes? See."

"See what?" Nelsa turned to Astarina and looked into those blue eyes. A tinge of sorrow stirred in her vital. As though a veil disappeared, she suddenly knew the truth. "No," she gasped. "It can't be. That's impossible. There's no—"

"They are your daughter's eyes," Salazano said. "I kept her safe all these years. No point in killing perfectly good stock."

"What are you talking about, Father?" Astarina said, bewildered.

"You…" Nelsa's entire body seethed forward at Salazano with rage.

"Uh uh," he said. "I'd hold off on killing me, unless you never want to see your daughter again. She might still be in there somewhere."

Nelsa stopped herself, clenching her teeth.

"I faked her death. Why waste a perfectly good

womb? She will be the vessel for my son to come into this world. My true heir. Rest assured, your son and their father are both still dead."

Nelsa punched him right in the nose. Then once more.

Salazano moaned and coughed. He spat blood and smiled. "Your daughter," he continued. "She had a purity to her that I could not deny. So I sent her to a safe haven in the Velutra where I cleansed her old life and moulded her mind to my desires. She is no longer your sweet Kayli, but my regal Astarina. My only regret is that I did not yet get the chance to put a child inside her."

Nelsa stared at her daughter, all grown up. Looking into those eyes stole all the air from her lungs. All those years of self-torment spent numb burned her vital with unfathomable regret.

Her daughter, her Kayli. Nelsa trembled.

Astarina scowled back in confusion. "What are you talking about?" she shouted. "Father! What do you mean?"

Salazano ignored her and kept talking to Nelsa. "You kill me, and I'll never release the memories of her childhood that I've locked away. The pure ones, of who she really is."

"You're lyin!" Maasi said.

"Tell me, Layli, am I lying? Does a mother not know their own daughter when they see her?"

"Kayli," Nelsa wept. "What did he do to you…Kayli…"

Astarina snarled and spat at her. "I'm not your daughter! I am the heir to the Salazano Family! Tell her you're lying, Father! Tell her!"

"Malleable things, the human mind," Salazano said. "Especially after so many years."

"But I took control of Ciro's mind," Nelsa stammered. "I should have seen that there, unless…"

"Unless I also corrupted his memories and all the others there. Except for Belva, of course."

"Why are you lying to her, Father?" Astarina cried. "Tell her the truth!"

Salazano only grinned.

Nelsa stepped forward and formed a pistola, pressing it hard against his forehead. "Give me back my daughter," she yelled. Her hand trembled. Her vital ached.

"Kill me and you'll never get her memories back."

"We destroyed his corpus, Nel," Maasi said privately. *"If the information was only on there then it's gone, but he could be hidin it somewhere else."*

"They weren't on my corpus," he said, as though reading their thoughts. "Nor are they stored in my own mind. They are kept safe in the Velutra, but only I know where."

Nelsa's mind raced. She ached for a drink of veroni to numb the disorder of her thoughts. "Tell me!" she screamed.

"Just kill him, Nel!" MoonKidd cried. *"We ain't got the time for this, we need to get out of here. Look outside! There's a caosin war goin on."*

"Let me live and I'll have the memories of your

daughter restored."

"There's no way he kept them after all this time," Maasi said. "Your daughter is gone, Nels."

"But I see her right here. Not now, not after everythin…"

"We're with you whatever you decide. But you need to decide quickly. We've got the drill lined up ready to break us out, but we need to go now."

Nelsa looked across into her daughter's blue eyes, the eyes of a stranger. She steadied her trembling hand on the smooth grip of her pistola and turned down to Salazano, the embodiment of all her sorrow, suffering and hatred. "My daughter is dead. You killed her. Now I will kill you."

"I will not waste any more words with your revenge," Salazano said. He held his chin high and closed his eyes. "I will prepare myself for the end."

CHAPTER THIRTY-FOUR

Restoring the Balance

An explosion ripped through the windows, sucking the throne outwards through a massive tear in the chamber's walls. Nelsa's stala kept her fixed on the ground but in through the wreckage came a mass of flying lawkeep soldiers.

"*Stow away your arms and no harm shall befall you.*" A hail echoed in Nelsa's mind from the warlif who first made the proposition. The deep commanding voice also boomed through the chamber. "Surrender! Don't fight!"

MoonKidd had already fired a burst of cryluns but promptly stopped at Maasi's command. The flying lawkeeps took a few hits but their black and red armour protected them. They didn't return any fire. The main gate suddenly rent open and more law flooded in, surrounding Nelsa and her friends in a circle of steady weapons. The gang shuffled closer together, but Marston and Maasi, who faced the missing throne, kept Salazano and Astarina kneeling on the floor. Nelsa remained between them, pistola pressed against Sal's head.

A man glided forward and down through the

wrecked opening. When he landed, he adjusted the red flower sticking out of a chest pocket on his suit and frowned. He wore his black hair short and his keen eyes had an artificial iris that glowed a bloody red. The man strode forward until he stopped right behind Salazano. "You're done, Sal," he said, voice raspy with contempt. "Finished."

Salazano scoffed. "What, Lecara can't even come himself, so he sends his pet?"

At that moment, a warlif leapt through, four tails flailing behind. When the tall creature landed, he unleashed a terrible howl as though the cosmos groaned. Through her stala, Nelsa's very bones trembled. When the warlif silenced the howl, he strode forward on all four towering limbs. The man stepped aside and the warlif stalked up behind Salazano, sniffed, and released a deeply distorted snarl.

This was the warlif Nelsa had made the deal with, although now he was wholly different. The warlif stood far larger than the one she had met, at least a head taller than her, and his long fur glistened in a black sheen except for a long red stripe that ran all the way down his spine and coloured the very tips of his four swaying tails. His large eyes were washed in crimson starlight. When he lifted his head back to its full height he pierced Nelsa with the force of his gaze, as though her mind and body were completely exposed and there was nowhere to hide. Her legs remained steadfast, as did her pistola against Salazano's head.

"Lecara," Salazano said. "This was all your ploy. A

truly ruinous one at that."

"Ruinous for you," Lecara growled. "You had me marked for death, foul serpent. So I employed our friend there, after I uncovered her past. Alas, it seems I still had to take matters into my own claws, though she and her friends proved a mighty fine distraction. They are quite well equipped, wouldn't you say? Chameleons to pose as bounty collectors, stala-piercing bolts, infectious programs to dismantle this chamber's grav-sheaths and using your horde of cryluns. Not to mention the use of that pure blinding blackness. Impressive indeed. All I expected was a coscraft explosion to claim your life and Layli's. I honestly hadn't expected any of this, but fortune would have my fangs rip your throat out after all. How delightful."

"No!" Nelsa objected. She dug the pistola barrel into Salazano's head. Fear of the warlif's wrath kept her from pulling the trigger. "He's mine!"

The warlif stalked around on his massive four legs, eyes narrowed at Nelsa as though she were his prey on a hunt. Maasi drifted out of the way after the warlif stared at the coavlen for a tense moment. He came to a stop beside Salazano and growled in Nelsa's face. "And who are you to give me commands?"

"I was about to uphold our deal," Nelsa pleaded. "Let me do it."

"Remove your weapon. Now. Or I'll kill all your friends."

"But—"

"Obey me!" the warlif bellowed.

Nelsa flinched at the noise, recoiling on instinct. Her pistola eased off. Lecara's paw whipped forward and clawed at her stomach, screeching against her stala and sending her backwards.

"Know your place," Lecara said.

Salazano snickered. "So, are you the only heretic or are the other Families just as disloyal?"

The warlif laughed like cracking thunder. Then he faced Salazano again. "Disloyal? It is by their vitals that I am given a warrant to remove your position of Padrino and dispose of your corporeal flesh, freeing this cosmos from your taint."

The warlif growled and snapped his jaws shut right at the side of Salazano's head. That silenced the suddenly old and frightened man. "The hunger of your lies and greed have outgrown the size of your stomach, rotten human! You have forced the other Families to spill blood for the sake of restoring balance to our home."

Still kneeling, Nelsa got back to her feet.

"We are the Four Families!" Lecara continued. "No longer shall we other three be under your wicked shadow. You forced this when you abandoned your honour long ago, Sal. The other Families have already decided on a replacement. The name Salazano dies with you. But don't fret, our honour remains. We'll give your dearly beloved Astarina a merciful death."

"No!" Nelsa objected. "You can't! She's my daughter!"

"What's this now?" Lecara said, amused.

Distraught tears leaked into her quivering mouth.

"He took her for his own and erased her memories, installing false ones. She was to breed him an heir. Please, don't kill her."

The warlif turned to Salazano and his maw curled up into a smile as his four tails softly swayed. "Is that so? I knew you were bringing a concubine here to solidify your reign, but not this. All your secrets and schemes are coming undone, Sal. How miserable you must feel right now. What would you have us do with Astarina, Layli?"

"Allow me to send her the memories I have of her childhood," Nelsa responded. "Give her the chance to know her real self and start a new life. Once she knows the truth she will question it all. I will take her into my care."

"I know who I am!" Astarina shrieked. "Father, why aren't you saying anything?"

The warlif chuckled deep in the back of his cavernous throat. "Your compassion is admirable, Layli, but a dangerous thing out here in the Frontier. Don't tell me you want Salazano to keep his life as well?"

"No," Nelsa said, turning from the warlif down to Salazano. She looked into his old, acidic eyes for a long silent moment. "I still demand my satisfaction. I demand his life for those he stole from me."

The warlif growled in contemplation. "Astarina cannot remain in the Frontier. She will be sent back to the Velutra. You may go with her, but not before you receive your satisfaction. Indeed the deal was for you to steal his life and you have upheld your intention to do so. I will give you this honour in light of the new beginning for the Four Families."

The warlif moved out of the way and Nelsa stepped up to Salazano again. She gripped her pistola tight, pointing it at his head.

"Not like that," Lecara said. "The demand for satisfaction must be resolved by a duel. I will see the Sacred Rites honoured."

"I don't want to duel him!" Nelsa cried. "I want to kill him now!"

She fired, but it screeched against a shield. The man behind it shook his head with an arrogant smile. Nelsa slumped and let out a heavy breath. "Please, just let me do this."

The warlif sucked in air through his sharp white fangs. "If you want me to honour my word and leave your daughter alive, you will honour the Sacred Rites. It is to be a duel to the death."

CHAPTER THIRTY-FIVE

Family

"Ten steps to doom," Lecara the warlif growled. "Sal, there is no victory for you here, but perhaps you can get revenge on the one chiefly responsible for your downfall. Spirata, conduct the Sacred Rites."

Still in the chamber, Salazano and Nelsa both stepped towards the man Spirata. In each hand he held out a black pistola, gripping them by the barrels.

"I award you both with a pistola formed from my own stala," Spirata said. "I will only permit them one shot. Only on my command will the duel begin. Only on the tolling of the bell shall each step be taken. You will each take ten steps while facing the other. You may only draw on the eleventh toll. Too soon and you will not be allowed to fire. You move to fire upon anything or anyone else and death shall befall you instantly. If neither is killed on the first duel, then we shall repeat it until one is victorious. Relinquish your stala to me, Nelsa. I shall provide you with the sacred duelling robes."

Nelsa acquiesced and the violet stala drifted off her body. As her robes crumbled away, a dark mist wrapped around her and solidified into black robes. The symbol of a white pistola gleamed on its breast. Salazano was draped in the same attire. They both took their provided pistola and stowed it in the new holsters on their hips.

"These duelling robes are for decency and the honoured tradition of the Sacred Duel," Spirata continued. "Aim well. They shall provide no defence to your single crylun bolt, nor shall you be given healing from any inflicted wound for a whole day after. If you try to remove the robes before that time has expired or heal yourself, then your life is forfeited. If the victor is not wounded then the robes may be cast aside, but if the victor is struck they must bear the wound for a day. Now, one of you does not have a corpus. What is to be done? Does one wish to relinquish theirs or does the other seek a replacement?"

"I seek no replacement," Salazano muttered. "What say you, wretch? Shall we see how good you are without that corpus aiding your trembling hands?"

Nelsa peered deep into his venomous eyes. "Once I'm in position I shall relinquish it."

"So be it. Take your positions." Spirata gestured to the two glowing circles marked on the floor some distance apart.

Salazano flashed a cold grin. "You should have killed me when you had the chance. You must know that I'm over two-hundred and sixty years of age, but there's something you probably don't know. I've been duelling since I was as young as Astarina, my daughter. Don't fret, I'll send you to your boy and your love in a moment."

He strode away. Astarina called out but he did not speak a single word, nor spare her a glance.

Unintimidated, Nelsa watched until he fell on his mark. Salazano stared straight ahead, gripping the pistola at his side. Her resolve was absolute. She turned back to Lecara and asked in thought: *"Do I have your assurance that my friends will be safe?"*

"Safe and paid," he answered, *"but should they cross me later then you will not think me much different from Salazano. Same applies to you, should you survive this duel. And yet I sense your desire to leave this world shall be fulfilled. Your words already betray you. Be content that if you fail to kill him, my fangs shall. Now get on with it. I enjoy such spectacles but I have more pressing matters to attend to."*

Nelsa turned from Lecara and took several steps to the left where her friends waited. They all stood at the centre but out of the duelling path, whilst other Lecaran gold guards scattered all over the chamber eagerly awaited the showdown.

"I'm sorry I lied to you all," Nelsa said, keeping their words private in thought. *"But how did you..."*

"I had me suspicions from the start," Maasi said, *"but I figured it out when I questioned if you were good right before you left. You ain't think I know you by now? You always forget I'm a coavlen and feel things you humans can't. Stealin this vague heirloom seemed a perfect cover to get to the real heist: Salazano's life. I told everyone after you left."*

"What about the bounty collector disguises, the coscraft and capturin me and everythin? You couldn't possibly have

planned all that in time."

"Wasn't much plannin, you're right in that," MoonKidd said. "More like a desperate gamble."

"I've had those chameleon disguises for quite a while," Maasi said. "As soon as you said Salazano had sent a projection in his stead, I knew we needed to get up there and rescue you from doin somethin stupid. Lo and behold, you did just that. I was tapped into their security so I could see and hear everythin happenin. The coscraft was all Jasolle. Ain't that right you mischievous illuavan?"

Nelsa looked around and only just realised Jasolle was not here but probably down in their hideout on Arkoma.

The illuavan's voice came to her mind. "We could not take the lawkeep coscrafts stationed down in the city up there. Any divergence from that would arouse suspicion, especially with everyone on high alert from the approaching heirloom. So we used a bounty collecting coscraft I previously purchased. I've got quite the graveyard waiting to be fixed. It just so happens this one was…somewhat still operational."

Marston's thoughts came next. "On our way up we decided that we were gonna just detonate the Blinder, snatch you up, and flee. But then you took the woman hostage and well, StarFlower of all people had the bright idea."

"We didn't make it in time before you was revealed," StarFlower said. "We were already in the bounty collector disguises. When I saw you tryin to escape I proposed stoppin you. Marston knew how to stop the life eater and you'd already told us that you were outta his special bullets, so there was no risk of you killin us. The risk would come when we *took you to Salazano and put him down for good."*

"But did you have to be so rough with me?" She grimly laughed in thought.

"Had to make it real didn't we?" Maasi answered. *"Maybe just a little was payback for keepin us in the dark. Anyway, I knew once we got inside I could take command of their grav-sheaths so they couldn't pin us. Marston's Blinder would give us the advantage, and I had the drill on standby to break through this chamber. The rest, well, you know everythin now."*

"We wanted you to get justice for your family," MoonKidd said. *"For the hurt he's caused us all. For everyone on Arkoma and beyond. Each of us has felt his greedy hands violatin our liberty. No more. You put this caosin cretin down, ya hear me?"*

"I hear ya," Nelsa said, looking down into the salenai's strangely concerned eyes. Then she turned to the translucent blue form of Maasi floating there like an otherworldly creature of a cosmic dark ocean. She looked through zais domed head to where Maasi's cryluss core—the heart, the being of the coavlen—and spoke aloud. "Thank you. All of you. I'm grateful to have such fine friends."

"We ain't ya friends, fool," Maasi said. "We're your family."

Nelsa smiled sadly. Then she moved over to Astarina, still tied up and kneeling by Marston. "You don't know how happy I am knowing you are alive."

Astarina scowled up at her then looked longingly at her father.

"I'm goin to show you the truth," Nelsa said. "I am your mother. I would do anythin for you."

"You can die," Astarina snarled.

Nelsa smiled brightly. "I can't do that, not anymore. I've got you to live for now. I'll bring you back, Kayli. I'll show you who I am. I'll show you your brother and your father. I'll show you how we were a family."

Nelsa closed her eyes and allowed the corpus to drain every memory still in her brain. She had nothing to hide. Nelsa removed the external corpus around her wrist and her mind darkened once more, then she commanded the stala down and around her daughter's arm.

"I don't want it!" Astarina yelled. "I don't want your lies! You can't force it upon me!"

"I'll show you everythin," Nelsa said. "Mars, release her."

Once the device re-solidified itself, Astarina gasped and closed her eyes. For several seconds she remained frozen and lost in a sea of memories before she shook her head and came back to the waking world. "It can't be," she muttered, clawing at the sides of her head. "No, it can't. Everything is a lie."

"I love you."

Nelsa turned and walked over to her mark, but the little flicker of joy on her face quickly crumbled into a grim expression. She did not yet face her enemy. Instead, she looked out the seamless window and beyond the castle. Flashes of battle still raged in the void, as did the sounds of fighting inside the castle, but Nelsa could sense them waning. Warfare was swift in this age. With the

Padrino unable to issue commands and presumed dead, the Sal Family was weak.

Nelsa focused her breath and connected to her body as best she could. She had a duel to win.

The ten steps to doom began in the Infamous Inner region of the Frontier half a millennia ago when the legendary outlaw StarTomb settled a dispute between two individuals demanding satisfaction. Each step forced the duelists to look into the other's eye, into the very essence of their being, their vital. They faced the reality of the precious strand of life that was about to be taken from the cosmos. When they took the final step, neither one fired. They'd realised their dispute was petty.

There would be no hesitation from Nelsa. She would kill her enemy.

"I sanction this duel," Lecara growled, his distorted warlif voice rumbling throughout the chamber. "I, Lecara Vadentia, of the Four Families. Satisfaction will be found in the eyes of the victor, whilst the loser will be returned to the Great Ocean Above or the black locker of Malnetha."

Nelsa closed her eyes, turned her head forward, and bowed. Then she straightened, opening her eyes to face her mark. Salazano's cruel eyes stared back.

CHAPTER THIRTY-SIX

Ten Steps to Doom

At the sound of the bell, Nelsa took her first step forward.

Nine steps to go.

Beside the great warlif Lecara, a short violet arch held a bell. Every toll sounded like the ethereal singing of a dying star, the ringing throes dying more each time.

Eight.

Seven.

Nelsa gripped her pistola firm. She would fire. Her resolve was as hard as senyar. But it was not a thirst for Salazano's blood that pushed Nelsa now. It was simply a desire to purge the world of this man's darkness. To restore some vestige of decency amidst the Frontier's degeneracy.

Six steps.

She wondered where this greater motivation came from, but then she remembered Kayli's face, all grown up. She wanted to make the world a better place for her daughter. There were so many things she never got to teach her children. Now, maybe one day she could.

Five.

The images of Colquin and Teec being slaughtered still raged in her mind. She breathed in, full of the complexities of human life. The mingled feelings of hatred, suffering, love, sorrow, and joy all burned inside her skull, in the very depths of her vital. She'd give anything to see their faces again, hear their voices and laughter, feel their embrace just once more.

The bell tolled again.

Four steps left.

Nelsa peered deep into Salazano's grinning eyes. They emanated malice, pride, detestation, honour and rage. All his thoughts were bent on killing Nelsa before he would have his long life cut too short. A sudden wave of pity for the wretched man washed through her. Her hand started to tremble on the pistola's grip.

Three steps to doom.

Her body ached with a longing for the numbing veroni. But her vital refused the craving. She would not hide the tragedy anymore. Instead, she clung onto the hope of a life yet to live with her daughter.

Two.

Nelsa managed to push all thoughts out of her mind and found a strange moment of peace. Her trembling hand stilled. She looked ahead, but in this quiet moment she didn't see anything at all.

The bell tolled again.

Nelsa put her left foot forward and took her last step. She gripped the pistola tight ready for the draw. Her focus returned to Salazano and his haggard grin heaved with hatred.

At the sound of the eleventh bell, Nelsa drew her pistola from the holster and flicked it up. She shot Salazano square between the eyes. It was done that quick. The corpse crumbled to the floor with a withered sigh.

As soon as Nelsa pulled the trigger, she gasped and the pistola fell to the floor. She placed a hand over her heart and felt the sticky warmth of blood. Another breathless gasp escaped her mouth.

"The victor is Layli Silnur," the warlif growled. But there was no applause, only hushed and grim murmurs.

Nelsa's knees buckled and she fell. The sharpness that bit her chest and the sensation of choking on blood left her struggling to breathe. Her body faltered and she fell backwards, but Maasi's tentacles caught her. Maasi stroked her forehead as zai gently laid her down.

"Let me heal her!" Maasi begged. To Nelsa, the coavlen's distressed voice sounded like the echoes of a dying melody. Over and over the words reverberated, gradually fading into silence.

"You know the laws," another voice said. Nelsa was too weak to care who it was. "She must bear the wound for a day hence. If you attempt to heal her then I will be forced to end her life before you can stop me."

Nelsa went to say something but coughed and sputtered blood instead. That did not stop her from trying again. "It's aight, Maasi," she stuttered. "It's okay."

"Save your words," Maasi wept.

"No," she said. "I ain't got much time left. I can feel my vital fadin real quick. Nothin can heal me now.

Lecara? Can you hear me?"

"A swift death you granted old Sal," the warlif growled. "It was more than he deserved. I can smell you are about to request something. What is it?"

Nelsa sputtered again, before continuing through wheezing gasps. "I need to get down to the planet. Give me a craft."

Lecara gave an approving snarl. "You wish to die where they did. Admirable. Spirata, see it is done and swift." There was a noticeable pause in the warlif's speech, as though in contemplation. "Do not heal her but make sure she does not die until then. And see to it that her friends are given the promised nomismo. They can have her share. But know this, thieves: if you cross me or the other Families again you will suffer a worse fate than Salazano." The warlif turned without another word, galloped away and leapt out of the chamber. Most of the other lawkeeps followed, though some lingered with Spirata.

Nelsa felt a strange relief from the wound on her chest, yet the feeling of being on the brink of death never left. Parts of her body were already numbed, though no veroni coursed through her limbs. She was glad for it.

"Mars, bring her to me, please."

Marston's binds lifted Astarina up and over to kneel beside Nelsa. Her heavy breathing slowed as she looked upon her dying mother. Her hands hesitantly fumbled forward. "You…you're…"

"I'm your mother," Nelsa whispered haggardly.

Kayli pulled her hands into her chest.

"It's okay. I don't expect your mind to grasp everythin now. I just needed you to know before I go. Spirata?" The man stepped forward. "Will you take her back to her coscraft? Send her to the Velutra."

"What if I don't want to go?" Kayli protested.

"You have no choice," Spirata replied. A part of his stala peeled off to bind Kayli again and he lifted her to her feet.

"Wait!" Kayli thrashed what little she could. "I want to stay with her! Let me go!"

"I will not have you watch me die as I watched you," Nelsa wept. "Just...just know that I love you. Find a better life in the Velutra. Spirata, take her. Go. I'm sorry, Kayli. I'll love you forever in the Ocean Above."

"Your coscraft is outside," Spirata said. "I gave command of it to the coavlen. Do not delay, for I will not hold your wounds for much longer."

"No!" Kayli cried. "Stop!" But Spirata did not stop as he moved her out of the chamber's front entrance.

Nelsa closed her eyes, trying to shut out her daughter's pleas. She opened them and looked upon Maasi, the pleas reverberating in her vital. "That was the hardest thing I've ever had to do."

"I know."

"I need to get out of here, Maasi."

"I've got you."

Nelsa turned to StarFlower, MoonKidd and Marston. "Will you rowdy lot join me?" she said. "I don't want to be alone when I go."

CHAPTER THIRTY-SEVEN

Sorry for the Delay

Nelsa lay bleeding in the sand where they died.

Dawn wasn't far off, merely a faint red glow on the distant horizons. The great black still choked the sky, scattered stars faintly singing of hope.

Maasi cradled Nelsa's head, whilst MoonKidd sat wrapped in the big arms of StarFlower on a nearby rock. Marston lay in the sand beside Nelsa, while Jasolle—who had travelled here as they descended to the planet—soft swayed behind them in the breeze like a pale green tree. His large eyes reflected the grief in his vital, a dull shade of mourning white.

"Just don't be doin anythin foolish," Nelsa said in a raspy whisper. Though her duelling robes held back the frigid night, she felt terribly cold, and became more still with every ragged breath. "You hear that, MoonKidd?"

"You know I cain't guarantee that," MoonKidd answered. "My lust for ismo is as bottomless as a Black Heart. One of these days I'ma go out blastin me pistolas against the backdrop of a dyin star." StarFlower pinched her shoulder and she added, "I'll do me best for you,

Nel."

"I'll keep her in line," StarFlower said. "I think we'll leave and get a fresh start someplace else."

"I know you will. Just be good wherever you go." Nelsa's weak laugh turned into a cough. Once it settled, she continued her farewells. "You gonna stick around these parts or head elsewhere, Jas?"

"The Frontier is always changing," Jasolle rustled. "The Velutra is ever creeping outwards, pushing us to new horizons. I wonder how long this world will remain before the Families feel the expanding pressures of the Velutra and it is absorbed. For me, I think it is time for a change. Perhaps I'll venture out towards the Schallas Frontier to find an unsettled world covered in forests, like my kind's homeworld. Living on this barren planet for so many years has done irrevocable damage to my vital. I miss the trees. I will depart to find them in hopes they provide me some solace."

"Thank you for everythin," Nelsa said. "You were there for me when I had no one. When I lost everythin. I will carry my debt to you into the Ocean Above."

"All your debts and all your sorrows will be absolved when you arrive," Jasolle rustled. "I am glad to have found you all those years ago, friend. Your life has had a considerable impact on my own, one I shall continue to carry until I meet my end. May Illuava guide you to yours, Layli Silnur."

Nelsa slowly turned her head to Marston, tears glistening down his cheeks. "And what about you, Mars? You gonna stick around here?"

Marston looked across at her with those wet eyes and she offered him a weak smile. "I cain't be the only one stayin behind," he said, voice firm despite his grief.

"Good," Nelsa said. "It's best you get out there, Mars. Stars are callin you for big things. I'll hold this planet down. But I need you to know that I lo—"

"I know," he said. Then he gently took her hand in his own. "I know."

Nelsa smiled a tear. She wanted to look into his eyes forever but could feel herself fading quicker. She tilted her head back to look up at the translucent dome of Maasi. "You best be moving on as well. Not trying to remind you of your cosless self, but I think it's time you moved on and finally found another human to try and bond with." She tightened her grip around Marston's hand. "I think it'll do you good to get away from all this nonsense."

"That so?" Maasi said with a short, crying laugh. The coavlen's voice became drenched in warped weeping. "Of course you're gonna spend your fadin words tellin me what to do."

"Should expect no less." Nelsa's eyes properly started shedding tears now. "I'll sorely miss you, Maasi."

"Aye," Maasi said. "You'll always have a special place in mah cryluss core. Forgive me, but what are you wantin done with your body?"

"They left their bodies out here to rot," Nelsa stammered. "Made sure to keep watch in case I came back. I could only watch from afar till one day not even the stains of their blood remained. They are somewhere still in these sands, lost. I want you to burn me where I lay. Let my ashes sink and drift away."

Nelsa turned back to look up at the stars and sighed. "Let me go Spirata," she croaked. The absent Spirata, feeling her intention through her robes, obeyed. Death landed back on her chest and she groaned in agony. "It's...about time Malnetha's locker caught up with me."

She no longer had the strength to keep her eyes open. Darkness folded in around her. "About time...I joined my family. I hope you can...find a new life, Kayli. One worth...livin. I'm finally comin for you, Colquin. Teec. I'll try my...best to...find you all in...the Cos Realm. I'm sorry...for the delay..."

The last thing Nelsa saw on Arkoma was a pale green river joining an endless ocean.

The last thing she felt was the warm embrace of all that once was and is.

The last thing Nelsa ever knew was that she had found her family again.

THE END

Acknowldgements

So many amazing people to thank, but first, as always, I must give recognition to my father, Michael. I wouldn't be where I am without him, I just wish he was still here. I can only follow that with a massive thanks to my partner, Hannah. She is the one that has to put up with my antics on the daily and somehow still loves me. To my Break-Ins family, thank you for always being there to support and cheer me on. Elisha, thank you for ripping this story apart and pushing me to be the best writer I can be. Your honest feedback has been invaluable on Arkoma and Dirge, I'm very lucky to have you as a friend and writing contemporary. Thank you Gracie again for your insightful edits and clearing up my incoherent ramblings. Everyone who gave their time to beta read Arkoma are absolute legends, thank you all much for your feedback on that early version. John and Rachel, thank you for creating another awesome cover, you've both outdone yourselves! To all my other friends, old and new, so glad to know you and have your support. All of you make all of this worth doing.

Review

Dear reader, you have my sincerest gratitude for giving your time to read this story. If I can ask only one more thing, it is that you leave an honest review on Amazon or Goodreads. Reviews are the best way to support indie authors so we can shine, but more importantly, so our stories can find their way into the minds of other readers such as yourself. These tales we write only live on in your memories, and by sharing your experience, they will endure. Thank you for your support, it means the world, I mean entire galaxy.

About the author

Born and raised in Australia, Calum Lott is the author of the Science Fantasy Duology: A Dirge For Cascius, Arkoma, as well as many other short stories set in the vast Valsollas galaxy. His greatest inspirations are the video game Bloodborne, the manga Berserk and The Lord of the Rings. In his spare time, you'll find Calum adequately playing the guitar, reading at a snail's pace, watching movies (LOTR over and over), annoying his gorgeous partner or sitting at his laptop writing stories whilst getting a sore arse.

WANTED DEAD OR ALIVE

NELSA NOLSTAR - Talented duelist rising in renown. Secretly a high class thief, lost in her addiction and the grief of her murdered family.

MAASI - A coavlen who takes on the appearance of a floating blue jellyfish. Zai is a talented nexbane: one who hacks systems.

MARSTON DEVETTA - A man of the Frontier. Marston is an expert with weapons, particularly explosions, but spends his free time tending animals.

MOONKIDD - An obnoxious salenai who has a short temper and is deeply insecure about her ancestry and height, but is fiercely loyal.

STARFLOWER - A large muscled human, calm even when in combat, which is often because he follows the lead of his best friend, MoonKidd.

JASOLLE - An illuavan born to the Frontiers, Jasolle had a rough upbringing drifting between worlds. He uses his wealth to help those less fortunate and to undermine the Four Families from within.

THE VITALS

HUMAN - One of the dominant sapient species in the galaxy. There is no end to the variety of human beings in this age as they are spread across a vast portion of the galaxy.

ILLUAVAN - One of the dominant sapient species in the galaxy. Tall and slender beings, with varying shades of green skin, and large lidless eyes that fluoresce with varying colours depending on their emotions. Together with the humans, with whom they are closely allied, they lead the civilization known as the Velutra of Valsollas.

SALENAI - A subspecies of humanity, salenais were forced to rapidly evolve over thousands of years during a genetic genocide. These altered humans have a small stout stature and reddish-brown skin. Their enhanced musculature makes the muscles appear as if they are on the outside of the skin.

COAVLEN - Artificially created minds whose forms are composed of a mass of cryluns—minute organic machines—and thus can take any form they desire. They enter the physical waking world from the non-physical realm of Norella, but those who choose to leave can never return. They will continue to live as long as they replenish their power source. They are genderless beings and thus are referred to as zai, a term derived from their true creators, the Zareiths.

WARLIF - Organic machine hybrid creatures who have been blessed with artificial sapience. The wolf-like warlifs were birthed thousands of years ago to aid in a terrible war that almost devoured the entire galaxy. They stand as tall as most human beings, grow more tails as they increase in age, and have specific types of weaponry embedded beneath their flesh and tough bones that make them terrible instruments of destruction.

THE NEXUS

CAOSI - A curse word derived from the disdain for the eternal force of Chaos, also known as Malnetha.

CHAMELEON - A device worn around a user's neck that projects a perfect disguise around the user's body.

COSCRAFT - A vessel that travels the vast distances between the stars by ascending to the higher dimension known as the Cos Realm.

COSTHRALL - The eternal force that gave birth to the cosmos and still gives it life. A non-sentient god that many, even in the Frontier, believe in.

CRYLUN - Tiny organic machines that can be controlled by a user's mind. When amassed they can form blades, projectile weaponry, armour, or anything the user desires. They also have the ability to swiftly heal wounds internally or externally.

CRYLUSS - The manufactured element that powers stalas, cryluns, coavlens and more.

VITAL - The essence of sapient beings that gives them their unique individuality.

FRONTIER - Any region outside of Velutran ter-

ritory where there is exploration, expansion and settle-
ment. Most regions do not obey Velutran Law.

GRAV-SHEATH – A sphere of manipulated gravity
used to move objects.

GRAV-TRAIN – Long serpent-like transports that
fly around a city, safely picking up and dropping off
passengers from the surface or other positions by casting
gravity sheaths.

LIFE EATER – A device that spawns a sphere of
nothingness, devouring everything inside.

LUMENSHIELD – A translucent energy shield projected around the user.

MALNETHA – Believed to be the other half of the
cosmos' creator, Malnetha is an eternal force of entropy
in opposition to Costhrall. Its decaying influence seeps
into the fabric of the universe and causes a madness
known as Mind Rot.

NOMISMO "ISMO" – The Frontier word for Velutran currency.

PADRINO – Salazano's self-imposed title to enforce
his power on the other Families.

STALA – A dense collection of microscopic crylun machines that permanently cover the user's body
with an imperceptible armour. Serve as clothes that can
change on command and rapidly heal any external or
internal wounds suffered.

VELUTRA – The strongest civilization in the
galaxy.

www.ingramcontent.com/pod-product-compliance
Lightning Source LLC
Chambersburg PA
CBHW010916090325
23042CB00005B/168